MW00943285

A DASTARDLY DEATH IN HILLBILLY HOLLOW

BLYTHE BAKER

Copyright © 2018 by Blythe Baker

All rights reserved.

No part of this book may be reproduced in any form or by any electronic or mechanical means, including information storage and retrieval systems, without written permission from the author, except for the use of brief quotations in a book review.

❀ Created with Vellum

DESCRIPTION

In the sleepy town of Hillbilly Hollow, the dead are waking...

When her cozy hometown is visited by death, Emma's investigative skills are enlisted by a secretive ghost. But with the uncooperative spirit holding so much back, and with the handsome local doctor pressing Emma for answers, will she ever get to the bottom of the case? Or will the Hollow be forever haunted by the secrets of the past?

CHAPTER 1

*M*y brain felt foggy as I woke, as if I were swimming through the murky waters at the bottom of Ford's Cross. I could hear a sound that was at once familiar and strange, muffled and far away. I forced myself to open my eyes and wake up. As I sat up in bed, the sound became clearer, and I knew where it must be coming from.

"Sugar!" I exclaimed, as I swung my feet around and hung them off the side of the bed. Snowball stirred and looked at me, getting up to follow me downstairs as I slipped on my muck boots and headed outside.

"Stay here, Snowball," I said to the little goat as I walked through the back door, and to the end of the porch. I saw the ladder peeking around the edge of the porch, and knew Grandpa was up and already on the job.

I could hear Grandma singing from atop the roof. She was having one of her funny spells again, sitting on the roof, singing to the chickens.

"Can I help, Grandpa?" I called up the ladder to him just as he got to the top.

BLYTHE BAKER

"Nope. I've got 'er," he called back down. "Just hold the ladder for me, Emma."

I did as he asked, and in just a moment, he was behind her as they both descended the ladder.

"Come on, Grandma," I said, wrapping an arm around her to ward off the evening chill. "Let's get you back to bed." I looked back to Grandpa and he nodded, picking up the ladder to take it back to the shed.

"Dolley's a sassy one, you know," Grandma said, seemingly randomly, as we walked into the house, her eyes a little glazed over.

I realized she was talking about Dolley Madison, one of the many chickens Grandma had named after first ladies. I didn't question the statement.

"I know, she *is* sassy," I agreed as I showed her into her and Grandpa's bedroom. "Did she have a falling out with Nancy again?" I asked.

"No, it was Pat! Can you believe it? She's usually so quiet!"

I guided her to the bed.

"Okay, Grandma. Lie down, now. Get some rest. You can sort things out between Dolley and Pat tomorrow." I pulled the sheet and quilt up over her as she put her head back on the pillow.

I walked back into the living room and Grandpa was heading toward the bedroom door. "Sorry to wake you, Emma," he said.

"Don't worry about it, Grandpa. It doesn't happen often. I'm just glad she's okay. Love you, Grandpa." I leaned up and kissed his cheek. "Goodnight."

I climbed the stairs back up to the attic with Snowball right on my heels. I had a lot to do in the days to come. Sunday was the last Old Fort Days event of the year until the Christmas Market started back up in November. I glanced over at my

2

dress, apron, and bonnet, hanging from the clothing rack. My re-enactment role was as a nurse when I was needed, though most of my work for the Historical Society was centered on creating flyers, and managing graphics for the society website. I had a couple of paying graphic design projects to complete as well. Suzy's wedding was coming up fast, and I needed to free up some time to help her with some of the details.

My eyes were heavy when I crawled back into bed. I pulled the covers up high, the bed warm, and the early autumn air cool in the attic I called home. Snowball trotted over to the edge of the bed, snuggling down on the little shag rug that lay on the floor beside me. I put my head back on the cool pillow, and snuggled down to get a few more hours of sleep before the morning.

* * *

THE WEATHER WAS GETTING COOLER, and it was time to start getting the farm ready for fall. Since I'd been back home, I'd adjusted to getting up at sunrise, and sometimes even before. With so many things to do on the farm, and everything else that I had going on, despite being tired from Grandma's late-night serenade, I was up before the sun.

I pulled on a pair of work pants, my muck boots and a sweatshirt. I wrangled my dark hair up into a ponytail and caught my reflection in the full-length mirror. I couldn't help but giggle. When I had lived in New York, my daily uniform was trendy dresses, cute jewelry and stylish heels. If the girls from the ad agency could see me now, they would die laughing.

Grandma had made some ham and biscuits the day before, knowing we would be busy but need a hearty break-fast for the day ahead. Grandma and Grandpa were already at the kitchen table when I came down. I grabbed a cup of coffee and a biscuit from the counter and sat down.

"Morning, Emma dear! Sleep well?" Grandma asked.

"I did thanks. You?" I looked at Grandpa who gave me side eye over the corner of his newspaper. He was the last person I knew who read the paper, cover to cover, every single day.

"Oh, I slept like a newborn babe." Grandma smiled. "So, how are Suzy's wedding plans coming along?"

"It's going well. I can't believe we have barely a week before she becomes a married woman. It seems like just yesterday we were walking the stage at high school graduation." I grinned, happy that my best friend had found her perfect match.

"Well, a maid of honor's work is never done! If you need any help, you let me know, dear." She patted me on the shoulder. "I hear that this event is getting bigger by the day." Grandma was clearly being fed information from the quilting circle, Hillbilly Hollow's own gossip chain.

She had a point, though. Suzy had started off saying they wanted a small, cozy ceremony, something simple with family and friends. Every week, though, the project seemed to grow. I had created adorable invitations and place cards for her, if I do say so myself. Mount Olivet Church, the oldest and largest church in Hillbilly Hollow, had plenty of room for a large crowd of wedding guests, and with its original and ornate nineteenth century bell tower still intact, it would make a beautiful backdrop for photos.

The reception, however, had to be moved from the fellowship hall due to the strict no-alcohol policy, which would have prevented the toast. Suzy had always dreamed of an elegant champagne toast at their wedding, and the Coltons were going to make sure their baby girl's dream came true. So, after numerous visits to reception venues and much deliberation, Suzy decided on the newly opened venue at Shaffers' Farm.

The Shaffers had put a lot of love and care into the old farm-turned-bed and breakfast. The latest addition to the property was the renovation of a massive, two-story barn that had been converted into an event venue. The place would have tables for dining and plenty of space for dancing. There had only been one wedding in the old barn so far, but with the newly renovated interior and strings of soft lights strewn overhead, the photos that Suzy had showed me of the space looked truly magical. Grandma's information from the quilting circle, at least on the transformation of Suzy and Brian's wedding from a simple family affair to the event of the year, had been accurate.

* * *

My FIRST CHORE of the day was winterizing the chicken coop. The beds needed to be insulated with extra hay, and lights had to be set up. The chickens would keep laying as frequently as they had in the summer if we set up lights on timers to fool them into thinking it was still summertime. When it got really cold, we would add some heat lamps, but that would be weeks away yet.

After the chicken coops were set up, I helped Grandpa clean out the chimney on the wood stove that heated the house. I helped him clean out the firebox of the stove. Since he had already been up on the roof the night before retrieving Grandma and knew better how to keep from making a mess in the house while we cleaned, I got up on the roof.

I was cautious as I stepped from the top of the ladder onto the shingles. I tended to be clumsy and didn't think a cast would be the right accessory for my maid of honor dress. Once I got up to the peak of the roof, I stepped toward the center where the chimney was located, and gained some confidence. I thought of Grandma sitting up here in the night, singing her heart out, and wondered how she was able to traverse the incline so effortlessly. I steadied myself above the chimney, and dropped the round brush down, twisting it as Grandpa had shown me. When he yelled up to stop, I went back down the ladder, feeling accomplished.

After cleaning the stove, I went upstairs and made a few phone calls. I had to make hair appointments for Suzy, her cousin Penelope, and me for the morning of the wedding. Suzy had mentioned that she liked how Cindy Green, who owned *Cinderella's Scissors* did her hair for a photoshoot she did for the local paper about her store, so I called and made appointments for the three of us for Saturday morning.

I also called Kipling Jewelers to check on her gift. I had gotten Suzy and Brian a fancy coffee machine as a wedding gift, but I also had something special on order for Suzy. Grandma had a photo of Suzy, Billy, and me from when we were about eight years old. I had a copy made and took it to Kipling's. John Kipling, the owner, was reducing the size of the image, and putting it in a locket for me. The inscription inside read, "one for all, all for one," something the three of us had said since we were kids to signify that we always had each other's backs. I knew Suzy would love it.

CHAPTER 2

On Sunday morning, I got up and donned my nineteenth century outfit to head down to the Old Fort. The ensemble was mostly authentic, though I did wear a small leather pouch slung across my body to hold my cell phone and car keys. Mr. Littman had called to let me know that they needed a nurse to fill in on Sunday. Sunday would be a full re-enactment day to wrap up the tourist season, with volunteers recreating the last big battle at Fort Harris.

I pulled in and parked the old farm truck around the back of the main building where volunteers were asked to park out of public view. I dropped my keys into the leather bag and headed to join the rest of the group.

Betty Blackwood spotted me as I walked up, and marched toward me, hands on her hips.

"Emma, is that rouge I see on your face? And mascara? That is not historically accurate," she said accusatorily. I hadn't heard anyone say *rouge* instead of blush in, well, ever. I knew that nineteenth-century nurses probably didn't typically use cosmetics, but hadn't expected anybody to notice.

"Sorry, Ms. Blackwood, but I had to have sunscreen, and

the mascara just made me feel a little more like myself," I defended.

"Hmpf! Next time, do try to keep your costume authentic, won't you?" She turned and stomped back off into the crowd, to scold someone else no doubt.

Mr. Littman was wearing his re-enactment gear, and he looked surprisingly natural in the navy-blue knickers, white socks, and blouson shirt. Perhaps it was because he was a history teacher, but the nineteenth-century gear seemed to suit him perfectly. He looked at his clipboard as he made his way through the crowd to me.

"Hello, Emma. So good to see you, my dear," he said, smiling broadly.

"Hi, Mr. Littman. Great to see you as well. What job do you have for me today?" I asked.

"Well, I'm afraid we are short a nurse, so nurse it is! Head on over to the medical building and they'll get you set up," he said with a smile.

At least I get an interesting job today, I thought.

There were so many people through the old fort that afternoon, I could hardly believe it. The weather was beautiful, though, and there were exhibitions of everything from soap-making to camp cooking. Periodically, some of the acting soldiers would wander in to the medical building for treatment. We would wrap them with strips of linen and send them on their way. Of course, there were a couple of actual medical issues as well. Mr. Lowery came in a little overheated after having spent too long on the battlefield. Mr. Jenkins came by as well, having cut his hand on the unfinished edge of a pan in the cooking demonstration. None of us were medical professionals, but we kept enough supplies on hand to care for any small emergency that might arise.

After a very long day at the old fort, I checked my phone to find I had a text from Suzy.

SUZY: Can u come over
ME: Just leaving the fort
SUZY: Pleeeeease! Bridal meltdown

Suzy had always been bossy, and could wear you down until you saw things her way, but given how stressed she was in these last days leading up to her wedding, I couldn't tell her no.

ME: Be right there

I got in the truck and headed to town. Suzy's shop would be closed for the day, so I went to her house instead.

When I arrived, she opened the door and burst out laughing. "You know, Emma, I see you in that getup just rarely enough that it still cracks me up every time. Little Emma on the Prairie!" She laughed hysterically.

"This is the thanks I get for rushing down here?" I laughed and shook my head.

"Sorry - you're right! Come on in," she said.

We headed for the dining room, which served as wedding central. There were stacks of bridal magazines, legal pads full of notes, and Suzy's tablet with inspiring pictures of weddings pulled up. Suzy's fiancé Brian was temporarily banned from the space. After they had made the major wedding decisions together, which could be interpreted as the decisions for which Brian had both the interest and the energy, Suzy wanted to plan some things on her own and allow Brian to have some surprises on the big day.

"Okay," I said as I flopped down in one of the dining room chairs, "what's the emergency?"

Suzy sighed heavily and sat down in front of her tablet. "Well, it's the dress. I'm stuck, Emma. I just can't pick." She was as pretty as ever, but there were dark shadows beneath her usually bright eyes. I knew the stress of planning the wedding and the anticipation of the day were wearing on her.

"Didn't we go through this weeks ago?" I asked. Suzy and I had narrowed her dress selection down to four of her favorites. I was under the impression that she had already made a final selection.

"Well…" She looked at me sheepishly. "I actually paid for all four, and said I'd take a refund on whichever ones I decided against." Her cheeks went a bit pink.

"Suzy! Are you nuts? I don't even want to know how much that cost," I said in disbelief.

Suzy wagged her hand back and forth in the air. "That's the least of my worries, Emma. I'm worried about what I'm going to look like on the *only* wedding day I plan on ever having. Geez, I've waited until I was thirty to tie the knot! I want to get it right," she said.

I realized how panicked she was and changed my tone. "Okay, okay. It's no big deal. We will figure it out," I said, standing up and stepping behind Suzy to look over her shoulder at the tablet. "These are the four?"

"Yep, that's them. Will you go with me tomorrow? I just want to try them all on one more time." She was looking up at me, and took my hand, just like she used to when we were little and something made her nervous.

"Of course I will." I squeezed her hand in mine. "One for all, remember?"

She heaved a sigh of relief and smiled up at me.

"I'm so glad you came home, Emma," she said.

"Me too, Suz," I replied.

CHAPTER 3

The next day, I finished the chores I had to do around the farm as early as I could so I could meet Suzy at Blush Boutique, the formalwear store in town, by our 2 pm appointment. Suzy had some nice dresses for an evening out, and even a few that could be cocktail wear, but Blush had full on prom and bridal styles.

We walked into Blush and were shown to the back of the store, where the bridal section was separated from the off-the-rack prom and evening-wear by an arched doorway covered with a heavy set of pale pink drapes. The area was beautifully designed. Phoebe, the owner, had run a large bridal store in Chicago before meeting Dan Rutherford when he was in town for a conference, falling in love, and moving back with him to Hillbilly Hollow. Phoebe had impeccable taste, and an odd knack for being able to tell before you even took it off the rack whether a dress would look good on your frame and figure.

"Hi, Suzy!" Phoebe said, air-kissing both Suzy's cheeks before turning to me. "And our maid of honor! Good to see you, Emma. Are you here to help our gorgeous bride here make her final selection?" Bright white teeth shone from between lips that were the most perfect hue of rosy pink lipstick.

"I certainly hope so! We're getting so close, I think it's now or never." I winked at Suzy.

"Well, Suzy, I have your fitting room all set up for you, and I took the liberty of putting some undergarments appropriate to the dresses in there as well. You *are* a 34C, aren't you?" she said with confidence.

"I don't know how you could know that, but yes!" Suzy looked at me, clearly impressed at Phoebe's fashion skills.

"Now, Emma, can I get you anything? Cucumber water? Or some champagne perhaps?" she asked me as she graciously flipped a perfectly manicured hand toward the large, cream-colored settee near the three-way mirror.

"Water would be great, thanks!" I replied and sat, waiting for Suzy to try on the first gown.

I flipped idly through my phone, and sipped on the refreshing bottle of cucumber water one of the shop assistants had brought over to me. After a few minutes, Suzy emerged in a long, slim dress with a trumpet skirt. It had a halter neckline, and an embroidered bodice in a filigree design. She stepped out of the dressing room, looked at me with her eyebrows raised, and stepped up onto the little stage that was in front of the three-way mirror.

"What do you think?" she asked, spinning around.

I cocked my head to the side, then stood up, standing in front of her to inspect the dress further. I crossed one arm over my chest, and rested my other elbow on it, tapping my lip as I considered the style.

"Well, on the one hand, it shows off your figure and you look a-mazing in that cut," I said.

"Thanks...but..." Suzy shrugged. She knew as well as I did this was not the dress.

"But, it doesn't *feel* like you, as silly as that sounds. If it were navy blue and you were wearing it to a ball, I'd say go for it," I replied.

"Yep, I'm just not feeling it. Just as well," she said. "This was the most expensive one. Okay, on to number two." She hopped off the stage and disappeared into the dressing room.

As I sat and waited for Suzy to put on the next dress, I realized there was someone in one of the other fitting rooms at the far end of the bridal boutique. Suzy had the largest, most luxurious dressing room, but then again she was looking at some of the most expensive dresses in the store. The bride-to-be in the fitting room at the far end was being attended to by a clerk who was periodically bringing in additional dresses, and telling her the prices, indicating she was someone who was not used to spending without regard to price. Still, I saw the assistant take in several of the higher-end gowns from the racks near Suzy's fitting room.

Suzy emerged in the second gown, which was a sleeveless sheath dress that went to the floor, with a plunging V-neck. She stepped onto the stage and looked at her backside in the mirror. "This one's not *bad*," she said, hesitantly.

"No, not bad." I looked her up and down. "You look amazing, obviously." Seriously, she had the best figure of anyone I knew, and her blonde curls made her look somewhere between Marilyn Monroe and Shirley Temple, depending on what she was wearing.

"It's just too...too...something," she replied, turning from the mirror to me. "Don't you think?"

"It's too New York. You look like you just stepped out of your Fifth Avenue penthouse," I replied. "It's not you."

She gave a small sigh, and disappeared once more into the dressing room.

Trying to see if I could spot a glimpse of the other bride, and wondering if it was someone we knew, I perused the dresses on the racks closer to the front of the bridal gallery. I saw a pretty one with a sweetheart bodice and a mesh lace overlay across the top and sleeves, and took it from the rack, almost absent-mindedly holding it up in front of myself in the mirror.

"You know," I heard Suzy's voice behind me, "we could be shopping for your dress, and it could be your big day we're planning if you'd just give a guy a chance."

I turned to find her standing in a strapless tea-length gown with a full skirt, her hands on her hips, smirking.

"What? As if. I was just killing time," I said, hurriedly putting the dress back on the rack. "Besides, I'm not dating anyone and there aren't exactly tons of eligible single guys in Hillbilly Hollow. Oh, unless you count the widowers down at the VFW." I gave her a smile that was dripping with sarcasm.

"There don't have to be tons. There's one, and he's the right one. A certain handsome doctor is absolutely crazy about you, Emma. And I think you're crazy about him too. You're just too darn stubborn to do anything about it." She cocked an eyebrow up at me.

"Um, no. Absolutely not. I've known Billy since we were in diapers. We've been best friends, the three of us, our whole lives. Even if I were…I mean if I did…if it didn't work out, I'd lose him forever, and I don't think I could stand that." I shook my head. I had too much going on to be getting involved with someone, not to mention something as complicated as going out with my best friend in the world.

"I know how stubborn you can be, Emma, but let me just say this. All this time – all those years you were gone, and he never dated anyone seriously. When you came back, it was like Billy woke up all of a sudden. He would never do anything to hurt you, but I've gotta tell ya, I don't think he'll wait for you forever. If you don't make a move, someone else will, and you might lose him forever anyway. No woman is going to want his first love hanging around even if she is in the friend zone." She rolled her eyes at me playfully, then grinned. "So, can we stop talking about your love interest for five minutes and talk about this dress?" She winked at me.

"Oh, by all means. Let's get off the topic that *you* started in the first place!" I laughed.

"So, what do you think?" she asked, twirling in a manner that befitted the full, playful skirt.

"You look like a princess…" I started.

"But…?" she asked.

"But a Cinderella princess, not the royal family kind. I'm afraid that one's a pass," I said.

"*Argh!*" She let out a noise of aggravation. "Okay, last one coming up, and if it's bad, we have to try on all of these," she wagged her finger above her head in a circle, pointing to all the dresses in the shop, "again, so brace yourself."

I sat back down and continued sipping on my cucumber water. Suzy had to let this matchmaking business go. I couldn't risk losing my oldest friend in the world. Although, she had a point. If he fell in love, got married even, she sure wouldn't want me hanging around. I thought briefly about the prospect of no longer being able to hang out with Billy and Halee, the best pup in the world, grilling burgers in the backyard. I thought about how he was always available when I called, unless he was with a patient, and how a woman in his life would change all that. I put down the cucumber water, suddenly feeling a little uneasy in my stomach.

Suddenly, the curtain of the dressing room at the front of the bridal gallery opened, and a woman stepped out, looking at herself in the large wall mirror. I could hardly believe my eyes. It was Prudence Huffler! Prudence, the mousy little organist from the Mount Olivet church. She had been in a bad way after Preacher Jacob had been murdered a few months before. People were genuinely worried about her.

The quilting circle ladies helped her mother, Margene, keep an eye on her around the clock for weeks. I had seen Prudence several weeks later at the Flower Festival auction when I bought the ill-fated banner that turned out not to be the work of Melody Campbell, but rather of her granddaughter, Mel. Prudence had seemed in much better spirits then, winning her bid for a banner I had originally had my eye on.

Today, there was no hint of sadness about her. She even looked different. Her skin, always having carried a bit of a sickly pallor, was bright and pink. Her eyes shone as she admired herself in the mirror, and the dress revealed a cute figure I had never known was hiding under her frumpy, matronly outfits. She smiled at her own reflection, not noticing me in the back of the boutique, and disappeared back into the fitting room.

A moment later, Suzy came out in the fourth and final dress. My mouth fell open when I saw her, and I knew there would be no need to try on every other dress in the store. It had a princess top, similar to the last one, but with a delicate lace overlay interwoven with the tiniest pearl beads. The skirt was a ball gown style, with layers of tulle underneath, and a taffeta overlay. The hem of the skirt had a delicate embroidered pattern that matched the lace of the bodice, with the same tiny pearls placed here and there throughout the design. It fit like it was custom made. Suzy was stunning.

She stepped up on the stage, and looked in the mirror, and her eyes immediately began to tear. "Is it – am I..." she started to ask, looking at my reflection as I stood behind her.

"Oh, Suzy! It is! You are going to be the most beautiful bride this town has ever seen. You look unreal." I realized then that my eyes were tearing up a little as well. "Honey, I am so happy for you!"

She grabbed my hand and squeezed it. "Am I ungracious

if I say I'm happy for me too?" We both laughed. "I'm going to marry the most wonderful man in the world, and I'll have my best friend beside me when I do. How did I ever get so lucky?"

Just then, Phoebe reappeared and said, "Okay then, go get out of it before you get mascara on it. I'll have it steamed out and it will be ready to pick up on Wednesday." She smiled.

"How'd you know this was the one I was taking?" Suzy asked.

"Tears, darling! If a woman sees herself in a dress and cries, she's ready to get married, and that's the dress to do it in!" She gave a soft chuckle.

"Now, as for you," Phoebe said, turning to me. "Let's try on your gown to make sure it fits properly and we don't need to make any alterations. It's in the fitting room next to Suzy's." She gave me a little nod.

I walked into the dressing room and as she had done for Suzy, Phoebe had hung appropriate undergarments next to the dress, and they were just my size. She was good. Suzy had decided on navy and silver gray for her wedding colors. I was appreciative, as the navy dress was one I could get away with wearing at a party or another event, not that there were many fancy events in Hillbilly Hollow, but one never knew, I supposed.

My dress, like the one for Suzy's cousin Penelope, the other bridesmaid, had a sweetheart neckline, similar to that of the dress that Suzy ultimately chose for herself. The skirt was a little fuller at the hips, with a slight gather, then tapered into a pencil shape toward the hem. I typically didn't wear anything completely strapless, but I had to admit, the color looked nice with my dark hair spilling in curls down my back, and I felt very glamorous.

"Come on out! Let us see!" Suzy called through the curtain.

I slipped into the heels that Phoebe had left in the room for me, also the perfect size, and stepped out of the dressing room.

"Oh. My. STARS, Emma! You look gorgeous, hon!" Suzy exclaimed when she saw me. "Step up and look in the mirror."

I stood on the little stage and turned around, admiring how the dress emphasized my modest curves, making me look ultra-feminine.

"It's pretty great, huh?" I said. "Great job picking it out, Suzy. I love it!"

"Great, now I have to invite Dr. and Mrs. Parker to the wedding," she said with a sigh.

"The dentist? Why do you say that?" I asked.

"Because. Billy's the only doctor in town, and when he sees you in that, he's going to have a heart attack, and I want someone with at least *some* kind of medical training on hand." She laughed hysterically.

I rolled my eyes. "Good grief, Suzy! You simply cannot stand to not get your way! So freakin' bossy! I might need to have a long talk with Brian and make sure he knows what he's in for!" We both laughed.

CHAPTER 4

*S*uzy and I had so much fun picking out the accessories for her dress, I had completely forgotten about Prudence until we were back at Suzy's shop.

"I can't believe I forgot to say something earlier," I said, "but you'll never believe who was at the bridal shop trying on gowns when we were there. Prudence Huffler."

"Shut up!" Suzy exclaimed. "Are you messing with me right now?"

"I am not. She walked right out of the dressing room in one, and was looking at herself in the big mirror. She never even saw me. She did sort of look over her shoulder toward the front a couple of times, like she was nervous. I was way in the back, though. She would never have known I was there. But you know what? She looked good. Really good. Happy," I said.

"You don't think...I mean, she took Preacher Jacob's death pretty hard. I didn't think she'd ever recover, if I'm honest. She couldn't have, I don't know, snapped or something, could she?" Suzy said tentatively.

"Surely not. I mean, the last time I saw her she looked in

much better spirits," I said, then a cold chill ran up my spine thinking of the *spirit* of Preacher Jacob who had visited me, not to mention Melody Campbell.

"Well, let's think about this, now. If she didn't snap, and we haven't heard any gossip about a wedding, that can only mean one thing." She looked at me as if I should follow her thought process and after a moment, I shrugged, having no idea what she meant. "A *secret engagement?*" she asked.

"No! You think so? But to who? I mean, I don't think I've ever seen her give anyone any notice," I replied.

"I don't know," Suzy said. "But I bet if we dig around enough, we can find out!" She clasped her hands together, rubbing her palms together like an evil villain.

"That was just a bit too enthusiastic, you know," I said.

"What do you want me to do, Emma? There's a limit to how much excitement Hillbilly Hollow has to offer." She chuckled.

"So, let's talk about something more fun! How are those honeymoon plans coming?" I asked.

"Well, Brian asked me if he could handle that to help out, since I basically kicked him out of most of the wedding plans." She giggled. "He told me to make sure my passport was up-to-date, and to pack a swimsuit! I'm so excited I can hardly stand it!" she said.

"Hmm, really? You do like to be in charge most of the time. You're okay with him booking a whole trip with no input from you whatsoever?" I smiled playfully.

"Kinda crazy, huh? I mean, yeah, I usually want to know everything. I mean, who are we kidding, I usually like to be in charge of everything. But with Brian…" She looked off for a moment and smiled. "I mean, I just know he's got my back. I have no doubt how much he loves me, so I trust him." She shrugged.

We chatted for a bit longer, and I agreed to meet Suzy the

next day at the bakery for round three of cake tasting. Brian had already weighed in on his favorites, apparently, and now it was my turn to give an opinion which I had no doubt Suzy would ignore only to make her own choice anyway.

* * *

BACK HOME, I had dinner with my grandparents and watched some TV before going upstairs. With curiosity getting the better of me, I decided to do an online search, and see if Prudence's name was on any registries, or even in an engagement announcement somewhere. If she were dating someone from the next town over, we would never know, after all, and who could say if she had met the love of her life after losing the man for whom she'd had unrequited love for so long. I shoved my curiosity to the back of my mind, and pushed through some additional work I needed to finish up.

I visited the freelance website to deliver my last two projects, and change my status to *on vacation,* when I found another job had popped through to my inbox. Worried about the time I had available over the coming days, I opened it to find it was a simple request for some custom wedding invitations. Fall weddings were in the air, it seemed. Lara, the buyer, was from Tampa, Florida, and sent me images of a couple of styles she liked, along with the details of her wedding, and a photo of her and her fiancé. She reminded me a little of a younger version of myself. She was petite with long, dark, wavy hair. Her fiancé was tall, broad-shouldered, and handsome with black hair and tanned skin. I replied to her that her order would be on the way shortly, updated my vacation settings, and was able to get her wedding invitations completed in no time at all. I even gave her a second design at no extra cost – my wedding gift to the adorable couple.

I closed my computer and stepped over to the window,

opening it to look out at the beautiful sky of the early autumn night. It was that perfect time of year where the days were comfortably warm, and the evenings were cool. I took a big lungful of fresh country air and smiled before closing the window and climbing into bed.

* * *

I SKIPPED my usual full breakfast the next day, knowing I would spend the afternoon at the bakery with Suzy tasting wedding cake varieties. I loved the bridesmaid's dresses that she had chosen for me and Penelope, and mine fit perfectly – I intended for it to still fit when Saturday rolled around.

Grandma had been canning the last of the summer fruit, along with some of her vegetable crops and making pickles all week. The manager of Farm King let the women's auxiliary set up a small booth outside the store on weekends to sell their homemade wares to support the local charities they sponsored. I helped her clean up the jars, add labels, and box everything up. I was going to drop them at the store when I went to town, where they would hold them for the weekend.

"Now, Maryann is going to mind the booth for us on Saturday while the rest of us are at Suzy and Brian's wedding," Grandma explained. "She drew the short straw, you know," she said, raising an eyebrow, "but she wasn't as close to them as the rest of us, not having had any children or grandchildren and never having been around you kids as much growing up."

"Will she be able to manage by herself?" I asked.

"Oh yes, she'll be fine. Lyndon, your Grandpa's friend, generously offered to help her. Mm-hm," she said, rolling her eyes and giggling. Then she whispered, "They're an item, you know."

I chuckled. "Yes, I suspected as much when I saw them

together at the Flower Festival." I remembered Billy grabbing my hand and dragging me over to dance beside Grandma and Grandpa that evening. They were looking at each other like newlyweds, as if there wasn't another soul around. Watching them dancing that night, I knew exactly what love looked like, and that was it.

Grandpa was coming in from the shed when we started walking out with the boxes full of jars, and when he saw us, he double-timed his walk to take the small box Grandma was carrying from her. As he took it from her hands, he leaned forward and gave her a small peck on the cheek. It was uncharacteristic for him, but every once in a while, he did some little thing that showed his affection. My grandpa was old-school. The strong, silent type. We never doubted for a moment, though, how much he loved us.

After we finished loading up the truck, I got cleaned up. I opted for a long-sleeved shirtdress and a pair of short boots. Not knowing what else Suzy would want to take care of, I wanted to be comfortable. I told Grandma that I would call her if I planned to be late, kissed her cheek, and headed to town.

CHAPTER 5

J pulled right up to the front door when I got to Farm King, knowing I had a lot to unload. The store was busy, which was no surprise, given that everyone was trying to get ahead of the cooler weather by winter-proofing their property.

I walked in and was surprised to see Dylan, Jennie Weaver's boyfriend, stocking shelves near the front. When Melody was killed a few months before, I had briefly wondered if Dylan could have been involved, since Melody had been giving Jennie a hard time at the diner. At that time, he was unemployed, having been laid off from the dog food factory, and rode his motorcycle around town, revving the engine at all hours of the day and night, much to the chagrin of local residence, and was hanging with a rough crowd. The Dylan I saw at Farm King, though, was completely trans-formed. He was clean-cut, wearing a button-down flannel work shirt, and khakis.

"Hi," Dylan said as soon as I walked in, "How can I help you today?" He flashed a broad smile.

"Hi, I'm just here to drop off some canned goods for the

women's auxiliary sale this weekend. I was hoping I could borrow a cart or something to bring them in," I replied.

"Oh, no ma'am!" Dylan replied enthusiastically. "Please, let me get those for you! Just show me to your vehicle."

I stepped outside and opened the gate of the truck. Dylan stacked two flats of jars, one on top of the other, and picked them up as if they weighed nothing. "These look great," he said. "I don't want to drop any, so I'll come right back for the rest." He disappeared into the store, and returned a few minutes later.

"Aren't you Jennie Weaver's boyfriend?" I asked as he got the next load of jars.

"Yes ma'am! Dylan – Dylan Shepherd." He stuck his hand out for me to shake. "And you're Emma Hooper. I've seen you around town. Nice to meet you properly, ma'am."

"Nice to meet you, Dylan. How's Jennie doing? I haven't seen her at the diner lately," I replied.

"Oh, she's great! She's working over at Mueller and Johns – the law office? She's a receptionist there now, and she's going to paralegal school online too. I got this job, and Mr. Plummer says if I do a good job, I might make assistant manager one day. In fact, I'm saving up to get Jennie an engagement ring, but don't tell anybody, will ya?" He winked.

Wow, wedding fever really was in the air. "That's great, Dylan! Congratulations!" I smiled at him.

After thanking Dylan for his help, I got back in the truck and headed over to Posh Closet to meet Suzy. Sweet Adeline's, the bakery, was just up the block so we could walk over for the cake tasting.

"Hi, Emma!" she said cheerfully as I walked into the shop.

"Hi, Suzy. Hi, Phoebe." I waved to the young woman behind the counter. She was a quiet girl, but very sweet, and most importantly for Suzy's sake, very dependable. "Suz, you ready to roll?" I asked.

"Yep. Let me grab my bag." She pulled a large purse from under the counter, and started toward the door, then stopped. "Oh! *And* my book!" She went back and retrieved a giant, 3-ring binder. It reminded me of those huge books that medical offices used to keep behind the counter with patient records when I was a kid before everything went digital. "Okay, let's do it!" she said cheerfully as she donned her sunglasses and we stepped out into the sunshine.

Sweet Adeline's had been in business in Hillbilly Hollow for nearly a hundred years. The same family, the Phillips, had owned it, one generation after the other. Diane Phillips was one of Grandma's quilting circle friends, but she had retired out of the business several years before. Her daughter, Alice, was closer to Suzy's mom's age, and she ran the place. She had kept all her family's recipes, but also added some modern twists. Like using the filling from their cream horns, a local favorite, in profiteroles to make beautiful, towering and impressive croquembouche, the French dessert, covered in lacy spun sugar.

"Come on through, Suzy. Hi, Emma," Alice said when we came in. "We've got you set up back here."

Off to the side of the bakery kitchen was a small room with a table and six chairs. It was decorated with paintings of cupcakes and sweets. We sat in the space and chatted for a moment with Alice, then one of the bakers brought in a small tray with slices of cake on little plates.

"No, not that one," Alice told the girl, "that one's for…" She stopped and looked at us. "That one is for the *confidential* client that's coming by this evening, remember? Suzy's is the large tray. It should be on the back prep table."

"Oh, of course! So sorry!" The girl disappeared and reappeared a moment later with a tray twice the size of the previous one.

"*Confidential* client, eh, Alice? What, did a celebrity move

27

to town, and nobody told us?" We both laughed heartily, but Alice's laugh was cautious.

"Oh, no!" She forced a smile. "Well, you know – we have to keep our client's privacy in mind. That's not just for doctors and lawyers, ya know. Bakers keep their secrets too!" She shrugged it off and pushed the tray the other baker had brought in to the center of the table before us. "Now, all these are labeled, and I've got a stack of forks and napkins right here for you. Suzy, is Brian joining you today?"

"No, I'm afraid not. He helped pick the venue, and a few details, and now he's concentrating on the honeymoon while I put the finishing touches on the ceremony. All he asks is that the groom's cake be some sort of chocolate." Suzy smiled.

"Well, there are four varieties there to choose from." Alice pointed to the far end of the tray where four decadent, brown squares of frosted bliss sat on little white plates. "If you don't like those, just let me know, and we can whip up something else. I'll check back with you soon!" Alice disappeared back into the kitchen.

"Do we really have to taste all of these?" I asked, pretending to be put out at the prospect of eating tons of cake.

"We do!" Suzy said cheerfully. "But, then we eat salads for the rest of the week!" She laughed.

Suzy pulled out two sheets of paper with little boxes all over them. "Here," she said. "We can rate each cake we try then compare notes. Write the name here," she pointed to the larger spaces, "then rate each one from one to five with five being the best and one being a pass."

We started sampling and I tried to be strategic, tasting the plainer flavors, like vanilla and white cake first, then moving on to stronger flavors, like chocolate and fruit. They were all delicious and I wasn't sure we would ever come to a consensus. White cake was traditional, of course, but Alice had told Suzy she could do a different flavor on every layer, with the small white cake layer on top. The tradition was that the top layer, the smallest one, was frozen and saved for the happy couple to eat on their one-year anniversary.

After eating cake until I thought I might be sick, I finally picked my top four, plus my favorite of the chocolate options for the groom's cake. "Okay," Suzy said, "you go first."

"Well, they're all amazing, but I think the Strawberry Shake, Perfectly Peach, All the Rage Raspberry, and then the Angel Wing White for the top. Oh! And Chocoholic for the groom's cake. How about you?" I asked.

Suzy squealed. "See? See why we're best friends?" She flipped her paper over to reveal she had chosen the exact same ones. "Heck, maybe I should be marrying *you* instead of Brian, you know me so well!" She laughed.

"First, quit trying to marry me off!" I laughed. "And second, you know blondes aren't my type."

"Oh, I know!" She gave me a knowing grin. "Besides, I don't think I could ever do better than Brian. I'm so crazy about him, Emma. I feel insanely lucky."

"He's the lucky one," I said. "You both are."

Alice came back and Suzy gave her the selections. We got up to leave, and my phone buzzed.

BILLY: Where r u? Haven't seen you in days.
ME: Wedding duty. Cake tasting

There was a pause, then he replied.

BILLY: I like cake

He followed the words with a frowny-face, and I giggled.
"Come on," Suzy said, "we have to go pick up the topper."

"Okay, we have to make one stop first, though," I replied. I turned to the girl behind the counter as we walked through the bakery. "Could I get one Strawberry Shake cupcake and one Chocoholic in a box please? Oh, and one of the Vanilla Rainbow in a separate box, too."

"You haven't had enough cake for one day, I take it?" Suzy asked, raising an eyebrow.

"I've had enough cake for a lifetime!" I said, then rethought my statement. "Well, that's a lie, but yes I've had enough for one day. We're dropping these off at the clinic," I replied.

We stopped by the clinic, where I gave the Vanilla Rainbow cupcake to Lana, Billy's receptionist. She told us to go back to his office to wait for him, and he appeared a few minutes later.

"Hi, Suz! Emma!" he said cheerfully as he walked in and sat down behind the shiny wooden desk. It looked like every desk in every doctor's office I'd ever been in. I thought they might be standard issue when a doctor received their medical license.

"Hi, Billy," Suzy said. "Is it a two-cupcake kind of day already?" She snickered.

"Oh, no," I interjected. "He cuts them in half, and smashes the strawberry half against the chocolate half and eats them together. Because he's a lunatic. I'm thinking of calling the medical board so they can have his head examined." I smirked.

"So says the woman who puts whipped cream on her hot chocolate instead of marshmallows. I don't know that her judgment can be trusted, Suz," Billy replied with a grin.

We chatted for a moment and made plans to all meet for dinner at Chez Jose the next night.

"I know I've been monopolizing her time, but she'll text

you later," Suzy said nodding in my direction as we stood to leave, "when we get back."

"Get back?" I asked.

"From Springfield. We have to go pick up the cake topper and the silver service." She winked at me. "Sorry, did I forget to mention? See ya, Billy," she said, walking out of his office.

"Is she wearing you out too much, Emma?" Billy asked.

"No, it's not so bad. I'm glad I'm here to do it with her." I shrugged.

"I'm glad too. Have fun in Springfield."

* * *

SUZY and I made the drive to Springfield in her SUV, which I had to admit was a darn site comfier than my old farm truck. It took us a little less than an hour, thanks to Suzy's lead foot. The small boutique where Suzy had ordered the custom cake topper and silver serving set was called *Merry, Marry.* It was located in the older downtown area. As we checked the GPS for the location, I looked up and saw that the Hotel Vandi-vort, where I had gone with Billy to the physicians' conference, was just ahead on the right. I thought about my talk with Dr. Edelson that night, and how much better I had felt about my experiences with spirits after we had spoken. I couldn't help but grin thinking about that evening.

"What's that all about?" Suzy swirled her finger in a circle in front of my face.

"Huh? What's what all about?" I replied.

"You know what! That look." She cocked an eyebrow up at me.

"Oh, nothing. Can't a girl just be generally happy?" I batted my eyelashes at her.

We soon found the boutique and Suzy did an amazingly

good job parallel parking against the curb. I fed the meter and we went inside.

The topper she had chosen was adorable. She hadn't yet picked out her dress when she ordered it, but as luck would have it, the dress on the bride figure was very similar to what she had ended up with. The bride had a blonde up-do, with a narrow cascade of curls spilling down the middle of her back. She had blue eyes, like Suzy's, and a huge smile. The groom figure, too, looked remarkably like Brian with neatly styled blondish-brown hair, and bright green eyes.

The serving set came from the same boutique, and was engraved exactly to Suzy's specifications. The hilt of both the knife and the server were engraved with a shield upon which there were several wavy, six-pointed stars. Around the shield was ivy which ran down the handle.

"The Bailey family crest," Suzy said proudly, showing me the intricate work.

After we finished at the boutique, we decided to head over to the Battlefield Mall. I was never much of a mall shopper, really, but it was nice to peruse some stores we didn't have at home. We ended up getting a mani-pedi, and picking up a few small things before we headed home.

By the time we started back, I had forgotten all about the mystery of Prudence Huffler's secret engagement.

CHAPTER 6

The venue at Shaffers' Farm didn't have any events before Suzy and Brian's wedding, so they had already started setting up when we got there on Wednesday afternoon for the final walkthrough Suzy had arranged.

Donna Shaffer, the co-owner, took us through, showing us where guests would park, where the band would be located, and where the photographer could set up. The wedding party table would be at the far end of the hall, with Suzy and Brian in the center, their parents, and the rest of the wedding party flanking them on either side. There was a table for the cake set up off to the side, and a gift table on the opposite corner.

Donna pulled me aside while Suzy was in the restroom to show me where the car would pull up after the reception. Brian had asked me to arrange a place for the limo to pick them up – the car to the airport for their honeymoon being arranged as a surprise for Suzy. Everything was in place for a perfect day.

As we were heading back to town, I got a call from Cindy Green confirming our appointment for Saturday morning.

She also let me know that the makeup artist that she sometimes worked with, Julia, would be available as well. I was glad to see that Suzy's demeanor was finally turning a corner from being nervous to becoming excited.

We met Billy at Chez Jose for dinner as we had planned. He had ordered an appetizer, which he had half-finished, by the time we got there. As soon as we sat down, we were surprised when Madeline came over with three glasses of champagne, which Billy had ordered for us. He held up his glass and said, "This might be our last meal together with all of us single. So, here's to you, Suzy, for boldly going where no musketeer has gone before! All for one!"

"And one for all!" Suzy and I chimed in, as we clanked the three glasses together.

Billy threw back the narrow glassful of bubbly quickly and grimaced. "That stuff tastes terrible. I don't know what you girls see in it." We all laughed.

We chatted only briefly before Suzy started doing the run-through of each of our responsibilities on her big day. Billy and I looked at each other. "Can we have the night off, boss? Just this once?" I asked, and he threw his head back and laughed.

Suzy looked indignant for a moment, then smiled. "Yes, of course," she said, rolling her eyes.

The conversation shifted, and we started talking about when Billy and I had met Suzy on our first day of kindergarten. "Remember," Billy said, "I was drawing with crayons on the easel and you came up and took the red crayon out of my hand and gave me a blue one and said, 'use this one instead.' Then Emma came running up to see what we were doing, and you took her by the hand and led her over to the other easel to draw with you."

"I had forgotten that!" I said, laughing. "You were even bossing us around back then!"

"Yep, and you were running to Billy's side, just in case he needed you. Even back then." Suzy smirked, and I saw Billy drop his head a little, his cheeks turning pink.

We were just about to order dessert when Billy's phone buzzed. "Oh no!" he exclaimed, jumping up and dropping his napkin on the table. "I gotta go! Call you later." He ran out of the restaurant.

"Wonder what that was all about," Suzy said.

"I don't know, but I hope everyone is okay."

* * *

THE ATTIC WAS GETTING COOLER, so I had swapped my typical sleep shorts for full pajamas. I was about to climb into bed when my phone buzzed. It was almost eleven, and I couldn't imagine anyone calling me so late – at least not anyone in Hillbilly Hollow. It was Billy.

"Did I wake you?" he asked as soon as I answered.

"No – I was just about to go to bed," I replied. "Everything okay? You ran out of the restaurant in such a hurry."

"Can you come outside?" he asked.

"You're at my house?"

"Yeah, I'm parked around the side. Meet me in the old spot?" he replied. When we were kids, he would always sit on a huge rock that sat around the side of the back porch closest to his house, waiting for me to come outside.

"Be right there." I pulled on my muck boots, went downstairs, and carefully shut the kitchen door behind me as I stepped outside so it wouldn't slam and wake my grandparents. Snowball reluctantly hopped up from her peaceful slumber to follow me outside.

"Are you okay?" I asked, worried by this time, when I saw Billy.

"Yeah, I'm okay," Billy said, reaching up and putting his

hand on my shoulder. "Emma, it's Prudence Huffler. Margene called Tucker out to Prudence's house this evening. The call I got was from him." He took a deep sigh, shaking his head, and continued, his voice deep and serious. "Emma, she tried to kill herself tonight."

"What!" I couldn't believe it. Prudence had been in a really dark place after Preacher Jacob had died, but she had seemed so much happier recently. "How? What happened?"

"Margene stopped by to bring her something she had baked for her, and she didn't answer the door. Margene used her key and let herself in, and found Prudence in bed, unresponsive. She called Tucker, and he called me from his car on the way. We arrived about the same time. She was still alive – barely – so we had the ambulance take her over to the county hospital."

"I don't understand." I didn't realize until that moment that tears were spilling from my eyes. Prudence and I weren't that close, but she was so young and I couldn't imagine her finding herself in such a dark place that she felt there was no hope. My mind flashed to how happy she had looked when I had seen her in the dress shop just days before. *Could she really have just snapped?* I had to wonder.

"She had taken some sleeping pills. I had given her a prescription for something really mild after Preacher Jacob died, but this was stronger – filled by an online pharmacy. I have no idea why she'd need those now. Anyway, she had obviously taken a lot of them. They pumped her stomach at the hospital, but I just – I don't know if she'll make it." He slumped down and sat on the edge of the porch, elbows on his knees, running his hands through his hair.

I sat down beside him and wrapped an arm around his back. "Billy, you couldn't have known. I know you did everything you could to help her – you're a good doctor," I reassured him.

"I just can't believe that I would be so out of touch...that one of my patients – someone I've known for so long, could be in such a bad place and I just didn't see it." He shook his head back and forth.

"You said they pumped her stomach at the hospital. Maybe she'll pull through. She's young...healthy," I offered, trying to help him feel better.

"Emma..." He paused, then turned to face me. "She's in a coma. The odds of her coming back from that aren't great."

CHAPTER 7

*A*fter Billy left, I sat for a while and thought about Prudence. I couldn't believe she would go so far as to try and take her own life. She may not have found the love she was looking for, and I knew she had been really down when Preacher Jacob spurned her advances, then died before she could try to change his mind. Still, she loved playing the organ at the church. She volunteered for several local charities, and was secretary of the Mount Olivet Church Historical Preservation Society. She had worked tirelessly to get the building on the Missouri list of registered historic places, and had finally succeeded. The early nineteenth century building was finally going to receive its official plaque, and be listed on the state guide to historic places. Now, it looked like she might not live to see her work come to fruition.

After tossing and turning for a while, I must have finally been so exhausted that I drifted off to sleep. It wasn't the crows that woke me the next morning, or one of Grandma's rooftop serenades. Instead, it was the sound of my normally calm sidekick, Snowball, bleating. I opened my eyes to find her on my bed, her nose inches from mine, as she bleated at the top of her little lungs. Having never awakened to the smell of goat breath, it is an experience I would highly discourage anyone from trying.

"What is your problem? And get your dirty hooves off my bed!" I gave her a nudge with my forearm and she jumped down. Still, she wouldn't stop crying. I rubbed my eyes and sat up, cross-legged in my bed. "Seriously, what is…" I stopped short when I looked at the foot of my bed.

Prudence Huffler was sitting on the edge of my bed, knees together, both palms in her lap, just as she did in church.

"Hello, Emma," Prudence said cheerfully.

I gasped. "Prudence!" I shook my head as if to make sure I was really awake. "Oh no, Prudence, no! You didn't make it?" I asked, tears starting to form in my eyes.

"Didn't make what?" Prudence asked, cocking her head to the side. When I had seen ghosts before, they had always been ethereal, diaphanous, and their appearance seemed tenuous. Prudence, though, did not look like the other spirits I had seen. She was almost translucent, but her color was vivid. She wore long-sleeved flannel pajamas with matching long pants. They were baby blue, and had a pattern of pianos all over them. Her brown hair looked the same color it always had, and the green of her eyes was a vivid emerald.

"Prudence, I don't know how to tell you this…" I had never before had to break the news to a spirit that they had passed on. I didn't know what effect it would have on her. "You were in the hospital, in a coma. You-you tried to end your life, Prudence, and if I can see you, that means, well, I'm afraid you've passed on. I'm so, so sorry!"

Prudence laughed, a small but hearty laugh with a little pig-snort at the end. Even in death the poor girl was not smooth.

"No, Emma! I'm not dead!"

"What? But….I can see you. You have to be dead," I replied, growing more confused. I wondered if she was in some sort of ghostly denial.

"No!" She waved her hand back and forth dismissively. "I'm in a coma. I was in the hospital, and everyone was making such a fuss over me. Dr. Will was there, and Tucker, and some nurses, and some doctor from the hospital was talking to Dr. Will. All of a sudden, it got really, really quiet. Then I heard a voice calling my name, so I got up and started walking toward it. I went out into the hall, and there was this bright light behind the door at the end, and that sounded like where the voice was coming from."

Prudence's story reminded me of those shows Grandma watched about people who had been to the brink of death, and lived to tell the tale.

"Anyway, as I got to the door, it sounded like my Granny Alene, but she's been dead since I was in high school, so I knew it couldn't be her. There was another hallway right before the doorway, and I walked down it instead. The next thing I knew, I was in your front yard, so I thought I'd come talk to you," Prudence said.

"Oh…okay." Most of the spirits who had visited me had a particular purpose. I wasn't sure how to make small talk with someone from the other side. "So, what did you want to talk to me about?"

"Well, when I was in my room, I heard Dr. Will say that I had taken some pills and tried to kill myself. I know you and he are close, so I wanted you to talk to him for me," she said.

"You did take pills, Prudence. You did try to kill yourself," I responded.

"No, Emma, I didn't! I would never kill myself. I don't know what happened. I remember eating steak earlier that night, then I got a phone call, and remember when I hung up I had a terrible headache. I don't remember a thing after that until I was in the hospital," she said, shaking her head, her brow furrowed. "You've gotta help me, Emma! I can't have people thinking I hurt myself. Especially Mama – she'll be devastated!"

"Okay, Prudence. I'll see what I can do to help. I can't exactly tell people we've talked though, unless I want to end up in the loony bin. You don't remember who you were with that night? Is there someone who might try to hurt you at all?" I asked.

Her brow still furrowed and her face bearing more concern, she shook her head again. "No. I have no idea who would want to hurt me."

Suddenly, Prudence disappeared and reappeared once, then again, like the picture on a television when the power surges. "What's happening?" I asked her, unsure if she would know any more than I did.

"I don't know. I feel strange." Her expression turned to one of someone who looks like they're about to be sick. "I think I have to go back, Emma. Please, just do whatever you can to find out what happened. Don't let Mama believe a lie about me. You're the only one who can help!"

"I'll try, Prudence, I promise," I said. I started to reach out my hand to pat her arm, and realized I couldn't.

"Thank you, Emma! Thank you so –," and with that, she disappeared.

* * *

I HAD a lot to do before I met Suzy at the florist, so I got dressed, and met Grandpa at the barn, where he was putting hay in the feeder racks. When it got really cold, the goats would eat hay instead of grazing in the snow-covered pastures, and they, along with other small livestock, would sleep in the barn where they could stay warmer. I had forgotten how much preparation it took to get the farm ready for winter. With Suzy's wedding just days away, and my new task of finding out what had happened to Prudence, my to-do list was overflowing.

Around six-thirty, I texted Billy. He opened the clinic at eight, but I knew he got up early every day to work out and go for a run.

ME: Hi. U get any rest?
BILLY: A little. Sorry I woke you.
ME: Don't apologize! all 4 1. I'll always b here 4 u.
BILLY: Thanks Emma
ME: Any update on Prudence?
BILLY: Just called hospital again. No change.
ME: Ok keep me posted. Wedding duty with suzy today. Text or call if u need us.

I finished with the hay, and Grandpa and I raked out the pig pen, and fed all the animals. I had to get ready quickly, having agreed to meet Suzy at her shop by eleven.

* * *

I STOPPED for coffee on the way, and gave the iced caramel one to Phoebe when I got to Posh Closet. "Thanks, Emma!" she said enthusiastically when she realized I'd remembered to include her. "Suzy's in the back."

I walked into the stock room, and went to Suzy's cozy little office in the back. "Wow, you're cutting it close," she said as soon as I walked in. "But, you brought coffee, so we're good." She grabbed a cup from the carrier and took a sip. "Emma, I'm not trying to be mean, but you kinda look like death warmed over this morning. You okay?" She was examining the dark circles that I knew were under my eyes.

"I had a late night and an early morning. Billy stopped by. We were up until after midnight." I sighed and heaved my shoulders, feeling the weight of my lack of sleep from the night before.

"Really?" Suzy asked, arching an eyebrow. "Is that a fact? Tell me everything and don't leave out one single detail." She put her elbow on the desk and propped her chin on her palm. I gave her a serious look and her demeanor changed to one full of concern. "Oh, sugar! You're not even playing, are you? What in the world happened?"

"Remember when we were having dinner last night and he got a call and had to rush out? He called me around eleven and said he was at my place and could we talk. I came outside and he gave me such awful news." I closed my eyes for a moment thinking of our conversation. "Suz, Prudence Huffler is in the hospital. She overdosed on pills and is in a coma."

"What? Emma, that's awful!" Her face was full of disbelief. "When did this happen?"

"It must've been late yesterday afternoon. Margene went to her house, and when Prudence didn't answer, she let herself in and found her in her bed. I can't believe it. It's terrible!"

"So," Suzy asked, "does Billy think she tried to hurt herself?"

"That's what he said it looked like, but I don't believe it. Remember? I saw her at the dress shop the other day when we were there for our dresses. She looked *so* happy, Suz! I can't believe she'd hurt herself," I said. Of course, I knew, from Prudence's early morning visit that she had not tried to commit suicide like people thought. I just couldn't tell Suzy about that. Seeing ghosts was bad enough, but if I tried to explain that coma patients were also able to disembody their spirits to visit me, it would be too much for anyone to believe.

"Sorry to share such bad news when we're in the midst of celebrating such a happy week for you," I said, realizing what a downer the whole situation was.

"No, I'm glad you told me. I'd feel like a total jerk if I'd been walking around oblivious. Let's just hope, and pray, that everything works out okay and she recovers. Miracles do happen, after all. Look what happened to you. That taxi that hit you in New York could've killed you, and instead, the accident brought you back to us, in a way." She gave me a sweet smile, and hugged me.

"You're right. We can't know what will happen. Let's go concentrate on something happy, okay?" I said, mustering a smile.

We went over to the florist to confirm the flower deliveries for the wedding, along with the flower selections for Suzy's bouquet, the bridesmaids' bouquets, and the boutonnieres for the guys. Suzy had chosen white roses with little embellishments of navy here and there. The clusters would be held with wide navy ribbon, topped by a narrow silver ribbon. The mockup the florist showed us looked beautiful.

As Suzy finalized the deliveries for the church and the reception, I went back to the cashier stand. I had decided to order some flowers to be sent to Prudence in the hospital. If, by some miracle, she did wake up, at least she would know people had been thinking of her, and I knew it would make Margene happy to feel like people cared about Prudence.

I decided on a bouquet of pink, purple, and yellow assorted flowers as the most cheerful choice. The clerk took my information, and Prudence's name as well. As she wrote in the delivery book, I noticed something unusual. There, just before my name on the page, someone else had requested a delivery for Prudence's hospital room. I didn't immediately recognize the name, so I squinted to make out the handwriting. *Peter Snipes.* I didn't know him, but there was a Snipes Funeral Home in town. I wondered if he was any relation to Mr. Snipes, who I had always known. I never knew him to have any children, though, so perhaps it was coincidence.

I wondered why this Peter Snipes, whoever he was, would be sending flowers to Prudence in the hospital. News always travels fast in a small town, but I couldn't believe so many people would even know what had happened to Prudence already. I pretended to be texting, and made a note of the name in my phone so I could look for some information on the mystery man later.

Suzy and I picked up our dresses and ran a few more errands around town before she dropped me off at her shop to pick up my truck. My ghostly visit from Prudence was gnawing at me, and I wanted to help her, if I could. I decided to go pay Tucker a visit and see what information, if any, I could get out of him.

CHAPTER 8

I swung by Sweet Adeline's and bought a couple dozen of their jumbo cookies to take to the Sheriff's office. I opened the box of treats to the deputy behind the desk, and asked to see Tucker. He grabbed a jumbo cookie and said, "Sure! He's in – just go on back."

I tapped the door frame lightly before walking into Tucker's office. "Hi Tuck, got a sec?" I asked.

"Hi, Emma. Sure, come on in," he replied, removing his feet from the spot on his desk where they had been parked, and taking on a more professional, police-like demeanor.

"I brought you and the guys something from the bakery. I understand it was a long night, and thought you could use the sugar," I said as I put the box of cookies on his desk.

He tipped the front of the lid up with his fingertip and peered inside. "Mm, snickerdoodle! My favorite! Thanks, Emma. That was awfully nice of you."

"Listen, I heard about what happened with Prudence. I just can't believe..." I paused, realizing that Tucker had no idea if Prudence and I were close or not. Maybe I could talk him into letting me into her house to look around. "I can't believe she wouldn't have told me she was in such a bad way."

"You two were close, then?" he asked.

"Well, yes. I mean, after Preacher Jacob died, I reached out to Prudence. I felt so bad for her, and wanted to help. I feel like I've just spoken to her, really." Okay, that part was not a lie, at least. I had just spoken to her, I just couldn't tell him that.

"I'm so sorry, Emma. I had no idea." He stood and came around to my side of the desk. He had his thumb tucked into his gun belt, and put his other arm lightly around my shoulder, patting me reassuringly. He really was a good guy, and cared about the people of our little town. I almost felt bad for tricking him, but I needed information, and I needed it fast if I was going to figure out what happened to Prudence.

"Things like this…" He shook his head. "They're just so senseless. I wish I could do or say something that would help, I really do."

"Well, maybe…" I paused for a moment, then continued. "I mean, I'm sure you can't – it's probably against all sorts of rules."

"Well, tell me what you're thinkin' and I can make that call myself." His dark blonde brows furrowed over deep blue eyes. Even when he was thoughtful or serious, he looked just a little bit like a cartoon superhero.

"Well, I was wondering…if I could just swing by her place, maybe I could get an idea why she was in such a bad place that night. It might help me, I don't know, deal with things better. But, I don't know, you probably locked up after you were there, and I'm sure there's some rule or something. I don't want you getting in trouble on my account," I said.

"Emma, you're forgettin' that I'm the sheriff around here. I can take you up there and let you in. I mean, Margene's known you your whole life, and it sounds like Prudence wouldn't mind." He gave me another pat on the shoulder and nodded his head reassuringly.

"Oh, thanks, Tucker! That would be great. Should I just follow you?" I asked.

"Yep." He walked over to the coatrack in the corner and picked up his hat, then slid his aviator shades out of his pocket and put them on.

"Taylor, I'll be back directly. If you need me, hit the radio," he said to the young deputy behind the counter as we walked outside.

* * *

PRUDENCE'S HOUSE was close to the sheriff's office. It was small, but neat and well maintained – exactly as I would have expected. I pulled my truck into the driveway beside Tucker's patrol car, and followed him around to the back door. He picked up the edge of the doormat and retrieved a key, then he used it to open the back door, and put it back under the mat.

Tucker, why didn't you just tell me the key was there instead of coming with me?

Sometimes I genuinely worried about the guy's ability to take care of even himself, let alone all of Hillbilly Hollow.

"Here you go, Emma," he said, holding the back kitchen door open for me to pass through. "Just lock up when you're done, won't ya? Again, I'm real sorry about your friend. I'll be prayin' for her. I hope you find what you're lookin' for."

He tipped his hat to me, and left.

I flipped on the kitchen light and looked around. It was clean enough to eat off of the floor, but I wasn't surprised. Prudence was always a very precise sort of person – it made sense she would keep an immaculately clean house. On the kitchen counter was a baking dish containing what looked like a banana nut loaf. It must have been what Margene was bringing over when she found Prudence. There were two clean glasses drying, upside down, in the dish rack, along with two small, white, round plates, and two forks. For someone who kept their house as tidy as Prudence did, it was strange to think she would have had two days' worth of dishes drying in the rack. She lived alone, so she must've had company the night she passed out.

I stepped through to the living room. A small, upright piano sat against the large, bay window near the front door. I could picture Prudence spending hours there, perfecting every note of *How Great Thou Art, Amazing Grace,* and *Oh Come All Ye Faithful* for her performances at church. The sheet music on the stand was unexpected, though. It wasn't another hymn but an old classic love song.

Could she really have been seeing someone that no one knew about? I wondered. All signs were beginning to point to a love interest of some sort.

I walked through the bathroom, and looked briefly in the medicine chest, but found nothing out of the ordinary. I saw the prescription bottle that Billy had mentioned. Most of the low-dose sleeping pills he had prescribed still seemed to be present and accounted for.

Next, I walked to the bedroom and flipped on the tall lamp in the corner. The bed was made, but clearly someone had been lying on top of the covers. A small quilt was pulled back as if someone had thrown it off and gotten out of bed. The pillow was dented, and the duvet disturbed where Prudence had presumably been lying when Margene found her. Next to the bed was a short glass that still contained about a tablespoon of water. The bottle which contained the pills that she was supposed to have taken lay on the bedside table as well.

Really, Tucker? You didn't think you needed to confiscate those as evidence?

I pulled a tissue from the box on the nightstand to avoid smudging any possible fingerprints on the bottle and picked it up.

Billy had mentioned that the stronger sleeping pills had come from a mail-order pharmacy. Sure enough, the online pharmacy was named on the bottle's label. There was also a patient phone number listed on the label. I made a note of the number, deciding I had better not call it until I had a better idea just what was going on.

As I put the medicine bottle back in its original location on the bedside table, something on the dresser across from the bed caught my eye. There was a photo of Prudence and Margene at Prudence's high school graduation in a wooden frame on the dresser. From behind it, though, I caught what seemed like a glint of metal. I pushed the wooden picture frame aside and behind it, saw a small, silver box.

It was about the size of a baseball, and looked a bit like a misshapen pumpkin. The lid had a black, braided silk tassel for a handle. I recognized the shape immediately. Among those I worked with in New York, it was common for young women to buy themselves a splurge when they got their first real job with decent pay. I had accompanied many of my friends shopping for their self-congratulatory gifts and they often came from the same store: Sampson & Sons Jewelers. I looked down at the ring on the second finger of my right hand. It was sterling and simple, with a distinctive organic shape, designed by Ella Pengrath. I would know her work anywhere, and the silver box was definitely her design, and definitely came from Sampson & Sons.

I used the tissue I still had in my hand to gingerly lift the lid. Inside was a diamond solitaire engagement ring. The stone in Suzy's engagement ring was large, and dazzlingly brilliant, but this stone was at least as big, and it bore the *Sampson & Sons* inscription inside the band. It had to have cost a fortune. I put the ring away, and carefully replaced the lid of the box.

I stood for a moment, baffled, looking around at the spare, conservative items in Prudence's cozy little home. Even if she had cracked and had some delusions of being engaged, she clearly did not have the means to buy herself a ring that required that sort of investment. She had to be engaged – really engaged – and to someone who was financially very well-off, for that matter.

In the living room, I took one last look around, and saw something propped up beside the sheet music that caught my attention. It was Prudence's diary. I thought it might help me figure out her movements in the days before she was hospitalized, so I tucked it under my arm. I walked back through kitchen, turning back just before I shut the door.

"I'm going to figure out what happened," I said, even knowing Prudence couldn't hear me. "If the worst happens, I won't let you cross over with your friends and family thinking you've done this to yourself. I'll find whoever is responsible, Prudence. I promise."

I shut the door, crossed to the driveway, and got in my truck.

$\mathcal{I}$ decided to go by the church and talk with Pastor Danny, who had stepped away from youth pastoring to take on the responsibility for the whole congregation after Preacher Jacob had died. I'd known Danny Baxter since we were kids. His older brother, Ted, was in our class at school, and had apparently dated Suzy for a while before she met Brian. I was sure Danny would be willing to talk with me about what had been going on with Prudence in recent days.

It was late afternoon, and I saw the SUV in the parking lot with the stick figures in the back window that I knew belonged to the Baxter family. There was a figure for Danny, one for Lena, and one for little Madison, their daughter. Lena, Danny's wife, had worked for Billy as his assistant since he had first opened the clinic. She had great organizational skills, and helped him keep the business side in order, and he gave her enough flexibility to take care of Madison as she needed to. It was a great setup for both of them.

I walked in through the front doors of the church. There were several older parishioners in the front pews, praying.

Careful not to disturb them, I quietly made my way around the back of the pews and up the side to the door that led to the offices. I found Rose Jenkins in the front office using a giant stapler to assemble some pamphlets.

"Hi, Mrs. Jenkins," I said. "Is Pastor Danny in by any chance?"

"Oh, hello, Emma!" She smiled sweetly at me. Like the rest of Grandma's quilting circle friends, Mrs. Jenkins had known me since I was born, and took a keen interest in every aspect of my life. She looked me up and down and I saw her tilt her head to look at my hands which were clutching the handles of my purse. As she led me to the door of the pastor's office, it occurred to me that she was looking for a ring. I didn't know what was in the tap water making everyone in town have wedding fever all of a sudden, but I made a mental note to drink only bottled water until it had passed.

"Pastor Danny, Emma Hooper would like a moment. Are you free?" Mrs. Jenkins said as she opened the door.

"Of course. Thank you, Mrs. Jenkins. Come on in, Emma." Danny stood from behind his desk, smiling, and made a broad arm gesture toward the seat across from him. "Please, make yourself comfortable. Can I get you anything? Glass of water?"

"Oh, no. No, thank you." I smiled and sat down.

"So, what can I do for you today?" Danny had a compact frame, but was fit, and neatly groomed. He wore his auburn hair parted deep at the side, and it always looked as if it had been combed through with some sort of product, it was so perfect. He wasn't as good looking as his brother Ted, but he had always been incredibly sweet and very studious. I wasn't surprised when I returned to Hillbilly Hollow to find he had become the youth pastor under Preacher Jacob.

"Well, I wanted to talk about Prudence, if I could," I said.

"Oh, I see." Danny sat back and put his elbows on the

arms of his chair, tenting his fingers together. "That is a very troubling situation. Very troubling indeed." He shook his head and make a tsk-tsk sound with his teeth. "When someone chooses to take their own life, we, who are left behind, can only wonder why they would feel so hopeless when there is so much love in the world to which they could turn to lift them up." He lifted his eyes slightly skyward on the last word.

"So true," I said, nodding my head. "That's what I was hoping to talk with you about. You see, I think something else might have happened. Prudence seemed so happy recently. It was almost as if something wonderful was happening in her life that the rest of us didn't know about yet. I just can't imagine her hurting herself."

"I know it can be hard to reconcile these things, Emma. I understand you not wanting to believe that she could feel that way," he replied.

It was growing obvious that he thought I was in denial. I had to try a different approach.

"Yes, it's hard. I wondered if there was anything here at the church upsetting her. I just need to wrap my head around the whole thing. Can you tell me if she was working on anything new? Maybe who she spoke to on Wednesday?"

"Well, let me see…she was starting to get the music selections together for the holiday choir practice which is starting up in a few weeks."

Mount Olivet Church had a longstanding tradition of caroling for charity, and Prudence led the special holiday choir. She selected the music, and conducted auditions for the coveted caroling spots.

"Oh, of course!" I said, as if she had told me about it and I had forgotten. "She was wrapping up auditions, right? Was there anyone she had to disappoint? I'm just wondering if delivering bad news to a hopeful caroler might have added to her mood in the days before…, well, you know."

"I'm not sure, Emma. She kept that list herself and I don't have a copy. I trusted her judgment, and knew she'd choose the best singers." He paused, looking out the window for a moment. "But you know, I did see her talking with Ambrose on Wednesday morning. I thought they might be talking about the music director position."

Ambrose Snodgrass had been the music teacher at the high school at one time. A bad car accident had left him blind, and he did piano tuning, and gave some independent music lessons in his home to supplement his income. I had never known him to be anything other than kind and friendly, and the poor man seemed to have a difficult time just getting from one place to another. I was sure he couldn't have even worked as a piano tuner if he hadn't already been doing it all his life when the accident occurred. It was second nature to him, though – a skill he hadn't had to learn. I couldn't imagine him hurting a fly, let alone trying to hurt Prudence.

"Music director? I didn't realize there was one," I said.

"Yes, well, there will be. With the congregation having grown in the past few years, and the church choir being asked to participate in some local events recently, the Board of Elders has decided to add another paid position – a Director of Music. Prudence has led the choir of carolers for several years and plays the organ every Sunday, but Ambrose had expressed interest in the position as well. He's been trying to get us to let him play the organ at Sunday service, but Prudence does a fine job, and we've seen no reason to change."

"Of course. Well, that just sounds like another opportunity for her to be excited about." I sighed. "I guess we can't know what happened. Maybe it was a mistake – perhaps she got confused and took the medicine more times than she should have. I just don't know."

"Well, all we can do now, Emma, is pray for her and those closest to her. I can see you're so upset by all of this. Let's bow our heads together, shall we?" He reached his hands across the desk to take mine, and I bowed my head as he said a few words for Prudence. I thanked him and left his office, but I left with even more questions than answers.

CHAPTER 10

*B*ack home, I excused myself right after dinner and went upstairs to see if I could find out anything else that would help me figure out what had happened to Prudence. I grabbed my phone, sat down at my laptop, and typed the name *Peter Snipes* into the search engine.

The first link to come up was for Snipes Funeral Home on Chestnut Street in Hillbilly Hollow. I clicked the link and went directly to the *About Us* page. The website outlined the history of Snipes Funeral Home, which was first started in nineteen-sixty by William Snipes, then passed down to his son, David. When David retired, he passed the business on to his nephew, Peter. Peter had been a mortician at a big funeral home in Kansas City that was one of a large chain before taking over the family business as Director of Snipes Funeral Home in Hillbilly Hollow.

The photo of Peter on the website made it look as if he was in his mid-thirties. He was an ordinary looking man with brown hair and pale skin but, in the photo at least, he had a kindly smile. I had to figure out why he was sending flowers to Prudence.

It was around nine, and I was exhausted, but I wanted to check on Billy before I went to bed. He had seemed like he was in such a bad way the night before, emotionally distraught from the events of the evening. I rang his cell.

"Hi, Emma," he said as soon as he answered.

"Hi, Billy. I just wanted to check and see how you were doing," I said.

"I'm glad to hear your voice," he said, his voice low and a little gravely, betraying how tired he was.

"I was worried about you, Billy. I know it's been a rough couple of days," I said. "Have you heard anything new?"

"No," he replied. "I called the hospital a couple of hours ago and they said her condition hadn't changed. I didn't tell you by text earlier, but I went by the hospital really early before my run. While I was there, her blood pressure dropped suddenly. She started to crash, and they administered epinephrine and used the paddles on her. After a couple of minutes, she seemed to…well, it was like she came back. She was still in the coma, but her vitals bounced back. It was a very close call."

I wondered if that was when I saw Prudence in my room. She had only been there a few minutes, and she disappeared so suddenly. I remembered her image seeming to flash in and out before she left. If my being able to see her was dependent on her body crashing, I hoped I didn't see her again. I couldn't help but hope there was still a chance she'd pull through.

"Billy, I feel like there's something you haven't told me. Are you *really* okay?" I asked.

He half-chuckled. "Oh, Emma, you always have been able to see right through me, haven't you? Well, you know I help out Tucker when there's a death – I'm usually the first person to be on-scene to examine the body. Unfortunately, losing patients comes with the territory for a doctor. I've been with some of my older patients, holding their hands, even, when they passed on. I've never lost someone as young as Prudence right before my eyes, though. I mean, she's Dr. Garrity's patient at the hospital now, but I've been treating her ever since I got my license and started my practice. She's still my patient. The idea of losing her with me standing right there, not able to do anything…it was bad, Emma."

"Oh, Billy, I am so, so sorry. I can only imagine what that must've felt like. Let's try to be a little positive, though, for Prudence's sake, okay? We only have a few days left before Suzy's wedding. There's still a lot to do. Did you get your suit yet?" I asked, trying to change the subject.

"I did." I could hear a little hint of a smile returning to his voice. "And I hear you and Suzy got your dresses as well. I can't wait to see them. I'm sure you'll both be beautiful."

"We tried on every dress in town, so I hope we look alright." I chuckled. "We can't have you boys outshining us, now, can we?"

We talked a while longer, and I agreed to come over for dinner the following night. I had to be in town anyway, and I sensed he could really use some cheering up.

I put on my pajamas, scratched Snowball under her chin, and got into bed. I laid my head back on the pillow, tired from a long day. I started to drift off to sleep, when suddenly, I sat bolt upright in bed. *Prudence's diary!* I had completely forgotten I had it. I went to my bag and retrieved the black, leather-bound binder. I turned on my bedside lamp and sat on the bed, putting my feet under the covers to stave off the evening chill. Of all the things I had brought back to make my room more home-like when I retrieved my things from New York, I had neglected to bring a space heater – a decision I regretted now the weather was turning cool.

I sat for a moment with my palm on the cover of the book. It was a huge invasion of privacy to read someone else's private thoughts. I wasn't sure I should even have the book, let alone be reading it. Prudence was still alive, after all, if hanging on by just a thread. She had asked for my help, though, and if there was something in the journal that would help me figure out what had happened to her, I had to do whatever I could to find it.

I took a deep breath and opened the book. Inside the cover was written Prudence Marianne Huffler with her phone number. *Her middle name is Marianne, and she goes by Prudence?* I had always seen Prudence as something of an enigma. She dressed very conservatively – more so than her mother, even. She seemed in one moment to be a little old lady trapped in a young woman's body. Then sometimes she did things, like writing her name and phone number in her diary that reminded me of a teenage girl.

I flipped through the first section, which I realized was a two-year, monthly calendar. There were dates highlighted for the Flower Festival, church pageants, choir practice, and other major local events. In June, there was a note on the day Preacher Jacob had died, bearing his dates of birth and death, which was circled. As I moved forward into early September, I realized that a weekly appointment became crossed out. I flipped back to the beginning. On Friday morning, about four weeks apart every month for the entire calendar was the word *hair*, written in pen as if it had been a long-term standing appointment. That would not have been unusual, except for the fact that, starting in August, every hair appointment was struck through in red, continuing through January. *Falling out with the hairdresser, maybe?* I wondered what could be so bad that a creature of habit like Prudence who hadn't changed her hairstyle since high school would fire her hairdresser.

On the first Saturday in September, the letters *P.S.* were written in blue ink, but then in the bottom-right corner was the tiniest little heart drawn in red ink. I had no idea what the p.s. stood for. *P.S., I love you? But who was it that Prudence had fallen in love with?* I went through and found a note from Tuesday that read *Adeline's 5pm.* So, maybe it was Prudence whose cake tray Alice's assistant had tried to give me and Suzy that day after all. In early November, a Saturday was circled in red, with no words included in the box. This was clearly something so important that she couldn't have forgotten what the appointment was, but something that she was excited for and counting down to. *Her wedding day!* It was all starting to make sense.

I flipped past the calendar and began leafing through the journal part of the diary. I paged through the entries for the prior year, but there didn't seem to be anything that related to present-day events, and I didn't want to disturb Prudence's privacy more than was absolutely necessary. As I went through the current year, paying particular attention to recent months, there was no mention of a fiancé or even a boyfriend. Instead, the pages were filled with speculative gossip about some of the townsfolk, and notes about things related to the church.

I finally came across something of interest, though, in the pages dated for last week.

MONDAY – Pastor Danny announced Music Director job. Can't wait!

Note: Start outline of music program plan, put together songbook for auditions, write up resume.

Tuesday – cannot believe they are letting Ambrose Snodgrass apply for Music Dir! 2-bit hack that has everyone fooled but I see right through him. When I get job will fire him and make sure I never have to see his smug face again.

Thursday – Unbelievable! Had all my music set out on the organ to practice for audition with Board of Elders. Ambrose came in to work on the organ, and suddenly my sheets were all missing. I went straight over to his house and confronted him but he said he had no idea what I was talking about. That a man employed by the church could tell such a bold faced lie just makes me sick.

Went back to church to practice some more and found all my sheet music in the garbage in the church kitchen, with a full bottle of soda poured in on top of them. Know it was Ambrose!

Monday – He doesn't know it, but I found a piece of sheet music on the floor after Ambrose was at church today. It was in braille, so I know it was his and is probably what he plans for audition. Moonlight Sonata for Piano No. 14. If that's the best he's got, I'm a shoe-in! Practicing a Chopin piece at home so he won't be able to hear what I'm working on.

So happy that everything is finally coming together for me! Music Director is in the bag, and with EVERYTHING else coming up soon, am happier than I have ever been. SO BLESSED!!!

IT WAS clear from her recent entries that Prudence was happy and positive, and definitely not in a mindset to end it all. I continued to read through the details of recent days, most of which were notes about music and activities – things she must have been thinking through or wanted to remember. I was about to put the book down and call it a night, when a note scrawled in the margin beside an entry for Tuesday caught my eye.

P.S. – check state records. history? license? CANNOT BE TRUE!

THE LAST LINE was underlined twice. I still wasn't sure what the p.s. notation meant unless it was her own shorthand for something. She was clearly planning to research something she was worried about, but I had no idea what it could be.

CHAPTER 11

I was thankful to wake the next morning without any visits from Prudence. The realization that she had only been able to visit me when her tenuous grasp on life was beginning to slip made my blood run cold. I wasn't sure what the mysterious notes in her diary had meant, but I knew I had to dig a little deeper, and I was afraid, with the wedding the following day and Prudence showing no sign of improvement, my time was running out.

I was excited to find that Grandma had made breakfast casserole. It was one of my favorite things, and she typically only made it around the holidays, or other busy times of the year. Knowing how much was going on with it being just one day before the wedding, she had made it just for me. The smell of ham, cheese and potatoes filled the air as I walked into the kitchen.

"Grandma! Thank you for making one of my favorites!" I kissed her cheek as I did every morning.

"Good morning, Emma, dear! Sleep well?" she asked, her face beaming with happiness as it usually was.

"I did, thanks! Busy days ahead today and tomorrow.

We're down to the wire for Suzy's wedding!" I replied, scooping a couple of spoons full of casserole onto my plate from the dish on the stove.

"Yes, it's all very exciting. She'll make a lovely bride," she said, then walked over and patted my shoulder. "But not half as lovely as you, dear. One of these days, perhaps. Whenever you decide you're ready."

I could always count on Grandma to love me and have my best interests at heart. She truly was one of the best people I knew. While everyone else was trying to marry me off, she was just worried about what was best for me. She sat with me while I ate breakfast, and we chatted about my dress, and Brian's honeymoon surprise destination for Suzy.

After we finished eating, I went to meet Grandpa in the back pasture so I could help him move the cattle to the smaller, enclosed pasture that was closer to the house than the summer grazing pasture. Rotating the fields from which the cattle grazed kept the grass from becoming too depleted in any one area. The other benefit of moving the cattle in the fall was the ability to move them to a grazing area that was surrounded by stands of trees, cutting down on some of the wind that could blow across the lower pasture in the coldest part of winter. I had a few more chores to take care of around the farm, then got cleaned up and headed to town.

Suzy had decided to forgo a traditional veil, and instead ordered a jeweled headband to wear with her dress. She had gotten combs for her cousin, Penelope, and me that were a similar style to her headband. I stopped by her house and picked them up.

"How's the honeymoon packing going?" I asked when she answered the door.

"Well," she said, breathing a heavy sigh, "It's pretty hard to pack for a trip when you don't know where you're going!" She laughed. "But, Brian told me to put everything aside that

I was thinking of taking, and he would swing by and tell me if there was anything I didn't need when he gets back." For Suzy to be letting someone else completely take over and make plans on her behalf it had to be true love.

"So, where is the groom today?" I asked.

"He went to Springfield to pick up the rings. Billy and Brad went with him. They were going to go out for an early dinner at some steakhouse he wanted to try before they come back."

I followed her into the dining room to pick up the hair accessories.

"It still seems crazy to me, ya know?" she continued. "I mean, in just two days I'll be Suzy Bailey." She shook her head.

"I know – it is really something! It's all coming together, though. It's going to be a beautiful day, Suzy. I couldn't be happier for anyone." I hugged her neck.

"Here you go," she said, handing me the box with the items to take to the salon.

* * *

CINDERELLA'S SCISSORS was a couple of blocks off Main Street on Sycamore. The building had been an older, craftsman style house, and Cinderella "Cindy" Green, a few years behind us in school, had converted the place into a salon several years before. Not only was there a hair salon, but she rented out a couple of the back rooms to other beauty practitioners. A nail technician had one space, and an aesthetician who did facials and waxing had another.

Although Cindy had to be making a pretty penny renting spaces out to other girls, she still did hair herself as well, perhaps just because she enjoyed it. Walking into the front room of the salon, the space was all pale pink with widely spaced black stripes on the walls. On the wall behind the front desk was a large, white oval framed in black with the Cinderella's Scissors logo in a fancy script. The entire space had a very girly and French vibe to the décor.

"Can I help you?" the very young receptionist behind the counter, who had blonde hair that faded into a bright blue color at the tips asked as I walked in.

"Hi, my name is Emma Hooper. I think Cindy is expecting me," I said.

"Sure thing – just a sec," the girl said, disappearing behind a pair of curtains that partially obscured the room beyond reception. She emerged a moment later. "She's just finishing with a client, but you can come back and wait if you like," the girl said, smiling.

"Thanks," I replied, walking through the curtains and taking a seat in a plush, cushioned chair that looked a little like a throne. Cindy, a pretty, auburn-haired woman of about twenty-seven, was across from me working on the hair of an older woman who looked a little familiar, but whose name I didn't know.

"So, what are you going to do about it?" the woman asked her as Cindy made her way around her, fussing at the tips of her hair with a pair of small scissors.

"Well, there's not much I can do," Cindy replied. "I mean, he never actually proposed, so there isn't much to do." Cindy shrugged.

"How long were you together?" the woman asked.

"Two years! Can you believe that? Two years and he just dumps me for some little church mouse. Unbelievable!" Cindy was clearly agitated, though I was coming in on the tail end of the conversation and was unsure of the details of what appeared to be her tale of romantic troubles.

"Well, honey, you can do much better," a woman in the

next chair, who was being worked on by a young, pretty brunette stylist replied.

"I appreciate that, but I just can't believe two years of my life are gone down the drain like that, ya know? And I mean, Peter has a great business, and we were going to have such a nice life together. Now here I am, starting my love life over from scratch, and having to fend for myself! And she had the nerve to keep comin' in my shop after they started up together! I mean, of all the absolute gall! She steals my boyfriend and then keeps comin' in for weeks like it was nothin'! Pete and I had only been broken up for a few days before they started seein' each other, from what I hear." She rolled her eyes and let out an annoyed sigh. "I mean, *if* I even believe that. For all I know, that low-down hussy was seeing him while we were still together!"

"Well, to be fair, honey, he's probably the first man who's ever paid her any attention," Cindy's customer chimed in. "I mean, she was in love with that preacher and he wouldn't give her the time of day."

My ears perked up. *Preacher? They had to be talking about Preacher Jacob, which could only mean that Cindy was talking about Prudence Huffler!* From the conversation I had been able to ascertain that Cindy had been dating someone named Peter who had thrown her over and soon started dating Prudence. They might be talking about Peter Snipes, the mortician who had sent Prudence flowers. *P.S.! He might be the person in Prudence's diary!*

"Okay, hon, I'm gonna let Sara rinse you out. Sara, can you do her wash?" Cindy motioned to a woman who was leaning against an empty hairdressing chair flipping through a hairstyle magazine.

"Now, I'm so sorry," Cindy said walking over to me. "I'm Cindy Green. How can I help you?"

"Hi, Cindy. I'm Emma Hooper, Suzy Colton's maid of

honor. I made the reservation for us for Saturday." I tucked the box with the hair accessories under my left arm and stuck out my right hand to shake hers.

"Oh, Emma! So nice to meet you," she said, shaking my hand with an enthusiastic smile. "I'm so pleased that Suzy chose me to do her hair for her special day!"

"I brought the hair jewelry we talked about. The headband is for Suzy, and the other two pieces are for Penelope and me," I said.

"Oh," Cindy said taking the box and opening it. "These are absolutely gorgeous! Turn around for me – let me see your hair."

I did as she asked and turned around, letting my dark curls drape down my back.

"Here, come sit in this chair for a minute," she said.

I sat down, and Cindy played with my hair for a moment, scooping up handfuls and placing it at different angles. "I think I'll do a half-updo for you. We can use the combs, and still get the effect of the curls cascading down the back. I've known Penelope for ages, and have done her hair before, so for her I'll do a simple updo. Suzy's will be back in the band, and down. You all are going to be gorgeous when I'm done with you." She winked at me.

"And the makeup artist will be here?" I confirmed.

"Yes, I have her booked. You're all set," she replied.

"That's great. I'll leave these with you, then." I handed her the box and smiled. I wondered how I could broach the subject of Prudence and Peter, and knew I'd have to do so carefully. "Listen, I don't mean to be nosy." I gingerly touched my fingertips to the girl's arm, mustering my most sympathetic face. "But I heard you talking about your man. I had something similar happen a few years ago. Did you know the other woman too?"

It was completely fabricated, of course, but if I was going

to get her to open up to me, I had to win her trust, and thought nothing would work faster than commiserating over a shared experience.

"I'm sad to say I do!" She shook her head. "I was friends with her – for years! Then before I knew what even happened, Peter was breakin' up with me, and datin' her!" She pursed her lips and crossed her arms in front of her. "So a word of warnin', hon, if you have a man you wanna keep, make sure he stays away from Prudence Huffler!"

"Wow," I said, feigning surprise. "I wouldn't have thought she was capable of something like that."

"Well, she came in here to get her hair done for years – since I first opened my shop! Now, though? I wouldn't spit on that cow if she were on fire!" Cindy said.

I had to find out if she realized what had happened to Prudence. If she didn't seem surprised, she might very well have been the person to hurt her. After all, there had been two dinner plates on the drying rack in Prudence's kitchen when I was there. She had clearly had someone at her house that she knew well and was comfortable enough to sit and eat with right before she became ill. That didn't mean, though, I supposed, that the killer couldn't have sabotaged her food or drink earlier in the evening.

"That's terrible, Cindy. I'm so sorry to hear it! But, you know she's in the hospital, right? In a coma from what I hear. They aren't even sure she's going to make it," I said, watching her reaction carefully.

"Whatever it was that got her there, I'm sure she deserved it!" Cindy said. "Hateful shrew! *Hmpf!*" She certainly wasn't surprised, but her expression wasn't smug, either. If she had been the one to hurt Prudence, she was definitely keeping her cool.

CHAPTER 12

I left Cindy's more confused than ever. When I had first talked to Pastor Danny, he had mentioned the professional feud that Prudence had with Ambrose Snodgrass, the piano tuner. They had both wanted the job of Music Director at the church. Ambrose seemed like a kindly, sweet man from what I could tell. Prudence's notes about his ambition for the job were in stark contrast to his outward appearance. Still, if he had been eking out a meager living as a piano tuner, the idea of the prestige and steady pay that came with the Music Director role might motivate him to do anything to get the job, I supposed.

After talking to Cindy, I had to wonder if she could have been angry enough to hurt Prudence. It sounded like Peter had a little money, based on her comments about him having a strong business. She had dated him for two years, so clearly, she felt something for him, and the idea of losing a man with a secure financial future may have compounded her pain. Could she have been angry enough to hurt Prudence, though? I wasn't sure, but I had watched enough crime shows to know that poison was thought of as a female murderer's weapon. It was clean, and could be administered with little intimate contact, after all.

I needed to run a few more errands, but my stomach was growling. I wouldn't head over to Billy's for dinner until later in the evening, so I decided to go to the diner and grab a bite to stave off my hunger.

The diner still had a handful of old stools at the counter which were popular at lunchtime. It was still early – not quite eleven. I had gotten up on farm time though, after all, and was famished. I sat down at one of the little stools, and Sherrie Selby waited on me. She hadn't exactly greeted me with open arms when I first came back to town. It seemed she had set her sights on Billy as a romantic interest for a while, and she had been jealous of our close friendship. Since I'd been home, though, she had moved on and now we got along well.

"Hi, Emma," she said as she set down a menu. "What ya havin' today?"

"Hi, Sherrie. Can I get a house salad with light dressing?" I smiled.

"Oh, right! Wedding tomorrow, huh? How's Suzy doin'? Gettin' nervous?" she asked, jotting my order down on a ticket and turning just enough to hang it on an ancient order wheel in the kitchen window that squeaked as she spun it around to face the cooks.

I chuckled. "Well, I think she's glad that the big day is almost here. In fact, I'm kind of glad too. I never realized how much work a wedding can be – even when it's not your own."

I sat for a few minutes, flipping through my phone as I waited for my salad to arrive. I suddenly heard someone behind me complaining to Sherrie. I glanced around to see Ambrose Snodgrass at the table behind me.

"I didn't ask for French fries. You're the one who brought

them. How am I supposed to know they were extra? If this place is going to start trying to rip off a blind man, what won't you do? It's despicable!" I heard him say.

"Mr. Snodgrass, you asked for them. I told you they were…" Sherrie started to argue, and he cut her off.

"No, no, no!" He smacked his hand hard against surface of the table. "I'm a poor old blind man, and you try to take advantage of me! It's not right!"

"Okay, okay!" Sherrie relented. "I'll go adjust the bill."

I turned back to see him smirking in response.

Hmpf. Maybe he's not a sweet old man after all.

After he settled his bill and left, Sherrie brought my salad over.

"You okay?" I asked.

"Hmm? Oh, yeah. I'm fine, thanks," she said, rolling her eyes. "Some of these folks practically make it a sport to get one over on the restaurant. What they don't know, or maybe don't care about is that all that counts against us, too." Sherrie shrugged. "But, what are you gonna do, ya know?"

I felt bad for Sherrie and left her a generous tip after finishing my small salad. I thought I had better stop by Suzy's and check on her, so I drove over to her house.

She didn't answer the door when I knocked, so I tried her cell, and there was no answer. I stepped back from the front door, and her SUV was still parked out front. I walked around the side of the house and peered over the wood slatted fence. No sign of Suzy. Walking back to the front door, I knocked again and still no answer. The door was unlocked, so I opened it just a crack and called out. "Suzy? It's Emma! Are you home?" Nothing.

I stepped inside the house and looked in the kitchen, and the dining room, where all the wedding planning supplies were still set up, along with a couple of wrapped gifts that must've been sent from out-of-town family members who couldn't attend.

All was quiet in the living room, so I walked upstairs to the bedroom. The bedroom door was standing open, and there she was, lying on the bed, hands folded on her belly, lying perfectly still.

Suzy! I was instantly terrified that something had happened to her. I rushed in, and grabbed her by the shoulders. "Suz! Talk to me!" I said shaking her.

Suzy's eyes flew open wide, and she began flailing her arms around. She startled me, and I stepped back, stumbling, and fell back, landing firmly on my backside with a thud.

"Sugar!" I exclaimed when my butt hit the floor. "Are you okay?" I asked her.

"Emma! You scared the fire out of me!" she said, sitting up and plucking earbuds from her ears.

I laughed. "I scared you? You scared me! I called, and I've been knocking and calling out. Why didn't you answer?"

Suzy giggled. "It's so silly," she said. "I was downstairs, going through some last-minute details, and all I could think about was what could go wrong. What if the flowers are all wrong? It' supposed to be warm tomorrow – what if the air conditioning goes out in the church? What if Aunt Deirdre has too much champagne and tries to get people to do the Macarena like she did at cousin Jocelyn's wedding?" She sighed, swinging her feet around so that they hung from the side of the bed. "I was getting really stressed about everything, and so I started looking up relaxation techniques. I found an app that lets you do a focused, uninterrupted meditation. I downloaded it, and popped in my earbuds to listen to it, and I must have dozed off!"

We went downstairs, laughing, and sat at the kitchen island to drink a glass of tea. "I get that you're worried, but really, when you really get down to it, what is tomorrow about?" I asked.

"It's about marrying Brian. It's about us both standing up and saying we want to be together forever," she said, smiling.

"Right. The important thing is you and Brian, promising yourselves to each other. The rest is just details."

Suzy leapt forward and threw her arms around my neck, hugging me tight. "You're right, Emma! You're so right! I feel *so* much better. Thank you!"

"You're welcome. Besides, maid of honor here, just doing my job," I replied.

"So, on to a more serious topic, I guess," she said. "Have you heard anything else about Prudence?"

"I'm afraid not. Billy said she's about the same," I replied, shaking my head. "I don't know, Suzy, the more I think about it, it just doesn't add up. I don't think she would have done anything to hurt herself. I am starting to think maybe someone was trying to hurt her."

"Really? I mean, I guess it's possible," Suzy replied. "I feel so bad for her, but if someone hurt her on purpose, that's even worse somehow."

CHAPTER 13

I still had a lot to do that afternoon, but decided, after talking to Suzy and starting to feel even worse for Prudence myself, that I would run by the hospital to check on her. If nothing else, I was sure Margene would be there and she could probably use the break from sitting by Prudence's bedside.

The hospital was right off of State Route 43, and serviced Hillbilly Hollow, and some of the neighboring, smaller towns, as well as serving as a central health care facility for people in most other parts of the county. Though the hospital was small, there were often both newly licensed and experienced doctors in rotation at the facility as part of their long-term obligation to their parent company, so the care was generally very good.

After navigating the twists and turns of the parking structure, I went inside and saw the woman behind the information desk for Prudence's room number. Typically, such information was not freely given, but the receptionist on duty was Lauren Selby, Sherrie's cousin, and had known me since she was in grade school.

"4123, Emma. Ms. Margene's up there with her now," Lauren said when I inquired after the room number.

"Thanks, Lauren. Really nice seeing you, though I wish the circumstances were better." I gave her a friendly look that was just short of a smile and went to the bank of elevators to find the right floor. Prudence was in a wing of the hospital reserved for people who needed special care. This was in part, I was certain, because of the coma, but also in part, I suspected, because she had come in as a suicide attempt.

I walked down the long corridor, the pungent scent of antiseptic wafting through the air. Prudence's room was about a third of the way down the first corridor I came to, on the left. When I walked through the doorway, I heard the terrible symphony of machines that was keeping Prudence tethered to life. Margene Huffler was sitting at her bedside, her elbows on the edge of the bed, and her head bowed down low, over her hands. It took me a minute to determine if she was praying or resting her head there, but after observing her, it appeared to be the latter.

I lightly rapped the edge of the doorframe. "Ms. Margene? Can I come in?" I asked. She whipped her head around, seeming surprised that someone was there.

"Emma? Yes, come in!" she said, standing, and looking at me with a mixture of surprise, appreciation, and confusion.

I walked in slowly, gazing around the room as I did. There were a few flower arrangements there, placed on a table near a fairly large window. Margene had opened the shades, allowing a stream of bright sunlight to come flooding in. It was a private room, which was nice in that it allowed Margene to spend time with her daughter without the distraction of other patients' family members coming in and out.

"Do come in, honey, and have a seat," she urged me again.

I walked to the foot of Prudence's bed and looked down

on her. She was not clad in the pajamas I had seen when she had visited me, but of course that had been days before. I spotted a large white bag with plastic writing that read *patient belongings* on a shelf, and imagined her personal clothing was there.

"Hi, Ms. Huffler," I said when Margene stepped forward to hug me. "I was just so sorry to hear about Prudence," I said.

"Thank you, dear. I just – I don't have any idea what happened. She was such a happy girl." I had put my hands on the foot rail of the bed as I looked Prudence over, and Margene patted my hand. "So full of life and gratitude. Now…I just don't know what's going to happen to her." She shook her head, and tears began to fill her eyes. I put a hand on her arm to try to give some semblance of comfort.

"How long have you been here?" I asked.

"Since they first brought her in, for the most part," she replied. "Your grandma came by, with Rose and Ethel. They sat with her for a while yesterday while I ran home to get some fresh clothes. I just keep thinking…you know, something could change, and I want to be here when she wakes up. I don't want her to be alone."

Margene's pale blue eyes were rimmed with pink, and she had a look of desperation about her. I had lost my parents as a small child – both at one time in a fatal car accident. I lashed out with anger and a complete lack of understanding as to how this could have happened to me – to our little family. As I got older, I sometimes thought of what it must have been like for my grandparents to lose them at a relatively young age. They never spoke about it, but little things, like the mark my father had carved in the support beam of the barn still being there, and the way my Grandma had talked about Mom wearing great-grandmother's jewelry at her wedding, told me that the wound was still fresh for them too.

"Who else has been by?" I asked.

"Well, Dr. Will has been a few times, and he calls to check on her every day. Pastor Danny has been by, of course." She said it as if the days had run together, and she was trying to recall who had been by, and when.

"I'm afraid I can't stay for too long, but why don't you go down to the cafeteria – at least get some coffee or a bite to eat. I'll sit with her for a bit." I nodded encouragingly.

"Well, I…I mean, if it's not too much trouble," she replied, "then that would be lovely, thank you. I'll be back directly." She grabbed her purse and headed out the door.

As I looked around, I was hopeful that Prudence wouldn't crash again, and make her spirit-self visible to me as she had done before. Fortunately, the machines that were monitoring her heart rate and feeding her fluids just kept beeping rhythmically.

I walked over to the flowers to see if they held any clues to her mysterious condition. I saw the arrangement from church, which was a modest spray of lilies and hydrangeas in a small cream vase with a cross on the front. The little arrangement I had sent was next to it, and beyond that was a large bouquet of assorted flowers which included some white roses.

As I looked at the arrangement, I could see a small card that had slipped between the plastic sleeve and the vase itself. I wondered if Margene had even noticed it, as it looked undisturbed. I pulled the note out and opened the card. It read simply, "I'm sorry." There was no signature but I wondered if these could be the flowers that were sent by Peter Snipes. If so, were the words "I'm sorry" a simple expression of sympathy or did they have some more sinister meaning? Exactly what might Snipes have to apologize for?

I poked around a little more, trying to balance my need to find clues to help Prudence with her need for privacy, but found nothing that shed any light on how Prudence got to her current state. I walked over to the side of the bed, and patted Prudence lightly on the shoulder. "I'm so sorry," I told her. "I'm trying, but I still don't know who put you here."

Margene re-appeared a few minutes later with a paper cup of coffee in one hand and a plastic clamshell container that held a piece of pie in the other. She glanced lovingly down at Prudence as she passed her, taking her previous place in the chair beside the bed.

"Thank you, Emma, for sitting with her," she said.

I stood and picked up my bag. "My pleasure, Ms. Huffler. I was happy to do it. Again, I'm just so sorry she's going through this. I'll be hoping to hear some good news soon," I said, waving goodbye as I stepped out into the corridor.

* * *

I HEADED BACK TO TOWN, needing to stop by Kipling's Jewelers to pick up the gift I was having made for Suzy. As I made my way through town, Main Street was blocked off just south of the little shopping center where the store was located. I pulled up to where Tucker had his car across the road, with his lights on. He stood in the street, diverting cars around the block. As I approached him, I rolled down my window.

"Hi, Tucker," I said. "Everything okay?"

"Hi, Emma," he answered. "Yeah, just a problem with the hydrant. Charles Phillips had a little mishap – swerved to avoid a ball that had bounced into the street from some kids playin' at one of the houses over there," he motioned to the houses across the street, "and when he swerved, he clipped the hydrant. Waitin' for the fire department to come shut it down."

"Oh, I see," I said. "At least nobody got hurt."

"Yep. You doin' alright?"

"Good thanks. Just came from the hospital – checking on Prudence. No change, I'm afraid," I offered.

"I'm sorry to hear that," he replied

I followed the detour around the back of the building, and along a small corridor that paralleled that stretch of Main Street. As I made my way along, I noticed someone leaned over into the dumpster behind the furniture store. The figure was looking into the dumpster and seemed to be choosing from several items inside before pulling small pieces of unfinished furniture from the dumpster and stacking them aside. With no one behind me, I pulled in to a space behind the building at the very end of the strip and continued watching the figure in my mirror.

Strangely enough, I had seen exactly this type of thing regularly in New York. There, with limited space and a high cost of living, people often lived by the mantra of one man's trash being another man's treasure. As I watched the person at the dumpster finish stacking up their finds and pick up several pieces to carry them back to wherever they came from, though, I saw that they also had some sort of stick in their hand. As I continued to observe the scene, I realized the person I had been watching was none other than Ambrose Snodgrass.

Ambrose was an older man and had been rendered blind thanks to an illness several years before. I had heard that he could just make out some large shapes and movement, but had no ability to see colors or details. But the person before me, walking with a chair, a stool, and a small side table in his hands as he made his way up the street was certainly not the helpless, weak old man that he had portrayed himself to be.

Earlier, in the diner, I had seen him treat Sherrie very badly over paying for a side that cost an extra dollar, citing his handicap as a reason for her not to take advantage of him. The man before me was in perhaps better shape than I was at less than half his age.

According to the diary entries I had read, Ambrose had been a sort of rival to Prudence, vying for the Music Director job at the church. I had initially thought there could be no way that a quiet old man, let alone one who could barely see at all, could do any harm to anyone. Now, I was starting to rethink that theory.

I sat in my car for a moment, considering all I had learned about Prudence's life, and those who could want to hurt her. Ambrose was now a strong possibility on my list. With Prudence the obvious choice for Music Director, having played the organ at church for many years and being so well engrained in the church's activities, he may have wanted to get the competition out of the way.

Earlier, I was surprised to hear Cindy Green talk about Prudence as if she were some man-stealing hussy. Granted, everyone knew that Prudence had been crazy about Preacher Jacob, and I had even heard that she had professed her love for him before his untimely demise. Still, she hardly seemed like the type to use her feminine wiles to lure a man away from his long-time girlfriend. She typically wore button-up blouses that were closed all the way up to the neck, conservative cardigans, and long skirts with tights or hose underneath. Even at the church's fundraising picnic, she had worn a pair of impossibly high-waisted jeans with a long-sleeved button-up shirt under her themed t-shirt depicting the name of Mt. Olivet. She was a dark horse as a man-stealer.

Still, I had seen Prudence happily trying on wedding dresses, and found a beautiful, large, and very clearly expensive engagement ring hidden in her house. If she were engaged, though, why keep it under wraps? After so many years of being single, and the pain and embarrassment of her unrequited love for Preacher Jacob, why not announce her happiness to the world?

With the coast clear and Ambrose no longer in my line of sight, I quietly turned on the truck and made my way to the end of the alley, turning the corner to park in front of the ice cream shop. I would stop at Kipling's to pick up Suzy's gift, then I had one more stop to make. If I was going to get to the bottom of what had happened to Prudence, there was one more person I needed to talk to. I was running out of time before Suzy's wedding the following day, and Prudence might be running out of time altogether.

CHAPTER 14

J walked into Kipling Jewelers and was greeted enthusiastically by John Kipling, the owner. "Hi, Emma! Good to see you! I've got your very special order all ready to go. Please, have a look around while I go retrieve it from the back," he said.

"Hi, Mr. Kipling. Thanks!" I smiled back at him.

Mr. Kipling had owned the jewelry shop in town as long as I could remember. He was a short man with a portly shape, but a jovial nature and a broad, easy smile. He always wore suit pants with a matching vest that was just a bit too tight for him, and wore at least three rings on each hand, plus a heavy, flat gold chain around his wrist. His hair was non-existent on the top, but thick and bushy around the back and sides, a look that was echoed by his mustache. He looked a bit like someone from the disco era who had been dressed up as a 1930s merchant.

I perused the shelves of watches, bracelets, necklaces, and earrings as I waited. In one corner of the shop was a display case full of class rings, above which hung a faded high school pennant with the logo of the local team, *the fighting buffalo.* I, myself, had gotten my high school class ring here. I had chosen a demure option that looked dainty, rather than like the traditional class ring, and had a navy-blue stone for our school colors of blue and gold.

As I passed by a case with engagement rings and wedding bands, I looked over the selection. I couldn't help but think of the beautiful Sampson & Sons ring that Prudence had hidden away. I wondered if even her mother knew about her secret engagement. After all, she hadn't said a word, but had merely mentioned at the hospital that her daughter was happy.

"Well, I see you found the case with our wedding selections," I heard Mr. Kipling say as he emerged from the back room, breaking me from my thoughts. "With Suzy getting married, are you looking at walking down the aisle yourself? I haven't seen Dr. Will in here, but I wouldn't be surprised if he popped in to see me any day now to do some shopping of his own, hmm?" He raised a bushy eyebrow and gave me a sweet, enthusiastic smile.

"What? Oh, no, no, no!" I said, shaking my head more vigorously than I intended to. I wasn't surprised that so many people in town thought Billy and I were a couple. After all, we had been inseparable most of our lives, and it was something I had heard often since we were in high school, at least. Still, it made me think about people's perceptions, and how what looked like one thing to the outside world could be something else entirely.

Billy and I were very close. Suzy was my best girlfriend, and always would be, but with Billy, it went even beyond that. Since I'd been home, I'd come to realize that I had cut him off when I moved away because I knew that if I'd stayed close with him, I wouldn't have been able to stay away. I would have found myself right back here after college. In the end, I was back here after all, and we had picked right back up where we left off as if not a day had passed. I had gone back and forth with some sort of crush on Billy for most of our lives, and we had certainly flirted since I'd been home, just like we always had. Dating, though, was not worth the risk. I knew that, and he certainly knew that we were no more than just friends, but to the outside world – to the people of Hillbilly Hollow who saw us on a day-to-day basis, the perception was that we were together. We saw each other all the time, did things together, and neither of us was dating anyone else. That perception was their reality.

The perception about Prudence was that she had an unrequited love for a man whose life was tragically cut short. She gave the appearance of the quirky, kindly young spinster who played the organ at church and dressed years beyond her age. That was our perception. That was not, though, her reality, as I had come to find out.

Mr. Kipling laughed one of those whole-body laughs that made his belly shake, and the buttons on his suit vest strain to contain him. "Oh, Emma! You're an educated girl. I know you've heard the phrase, *'me thinks she doth protest too much'*! I was just having a little fun. I'm sorry." He raked the back of his chubby hand across his face, wiping under his eye as if he had told the funniest joke on the planet.

"No, it's okay." I chuckled and shrugged. "People often make that mistake, but we're just friends. Besides, it's Suzy's big day tomorrow – as her maid of honor, that's all I'm really focused on right now." I smiled.

"Well, you are a good friend, indeed. In fact, I don't remember a time when I didn't see you, Suzy, and little Billy, as we all called him back then, together. It must be good to have such strong friendships – the kind that last a lifetime!" He nodded affably. He was right. I was incredibly lucky to have them back in my life and I was suddenly overwhelmed by the idea I should tell them that more often.

"Okay then, let's have a look at this locket, shall we? Michael, my apprentice – you might remember him…my cousin Mildred's son? Anyway, he's a very talented artist, you know. Take a look at the engraving work and tell me what you think. I have a loupe here if you'd like to use it for a closer look. Like this." He demonstrated for me, and set the loupe down upon a large, black velvet cloth he had laid out on the countertop.

I picked up the silver locket and held it in my hand. The size was perfect – large enough to be visible but not so big as to be show-y. The silver chain was delicate and feminine, and the engraved design on the outside of the silver locket was intricate and beautiful. I opened it, and inside was the picture of the three of us. We were probably eight or nine, and judging by the t-shirts we wore, it was summertime. I was surprised when I first saw the photo, as our faces were each a bit dirty, particularly at the sides of our mouths where dirt stuck to what I could only presume was some sort of food we had recently consumed. Ice cream? Watermelon? It was diffi-cult to say what it might have been. It was unlike our parents and grandparents to allow a photo to be taken with us in such a state, but we had clearly been having fun, and whoever took the photo saw the opportunity for just what it was: a chance to capture us in a happy and free moment of our childhood.

Billy stood up straight in the background, just a little taller than Suzy and me, with his shoulders squared. His black hair was thick, and his eyes dark against his tanned skin. Even as a little boy he was handsome. I was leaned up against him, my shoulder resting against his. I was tanned from a summer of playing outdoors, but never got to be anything like the golden color Billy so easily achieved with his Cherokee heritage. My dark hair was a mess, with wild, stray hairs sticking out here and there from the two braids that tried to contain my wayward curls. Between us, standing just in front of us, was Suzy. Her hands were on her hips, her chin raised as she looked confidently at the camera, her blue eyes piercing, daring any onlooker to challenge her.

I felt a single tear breach my bottom lashes, and quickly wiped it away with the back of my finger as I read the inscription. In beautiful, scripted font across from our photo read our motto, *one for all and all for one.* "Oh, Mr. Kipling! It's just beautiful!" I said, my voice betraying a little emotion.

The expert salesman smiled proudly, and quickly produced a box of tissues from under the counter, offering me one. "I'm so happy you're pleased, Emma. I truly am. Michael will be thrilled that you like his work so well." He smiled and nodded.

We made small talk while he polished up the locket, removing my fingerprints and any smudges, and packaged it up for me with a lovely box and ribbon. "So, Mr. Kipling, about these wedding sets," I said, my eyes going to a tray of wedding bands and engagement rings that seemed to be a hodge-podge of different styles, quality, and price points. "And again," I smiled playfully, "I'm not asking for me, but… are these pre-owned or something?"

He chuckled, never putting his work down as we talked. "Oh, yes, very good eye! Some of those are designer, some are from department stores. We typically deal in new and original pieces, but sometimes people come through wanting to liquidate a piece, or a set. Perhaps the marriage has, tragically, ended, or the wedding fell through altogether. I am not really set up as a buyer, mind you, but I do buy things on occasion if the piece is a good addition to our inventory, or more often than not, just to help someone out."

He smiled. He did not want to be thought of as a pawn shop or second-hand store, I was certain, but judging by the glistening gemstones of the rings he wore himself, I was also certain that he was a shrewd businessman and would not turn down a good business deal when he saw one.

"Say," I continued as I looked through the case, "you don't ever get things from Sampson & Sons, by chance, do you?"

"Funny you should mention! I had a beautiful Sampson solitaire sitting here for ages, actually. I took it in along with a beautiful silver box from a lovely woman who was passing through on her way out west. Her husband, she realized, had a penchant for the ladies, and she was heading to California to live with her sister. Along the way, she had looked down at the ring, and decided right then and there that she never wanted to see it again, so when she stopped in town for lunch, she came and saw me, and sold it to me, along with the silver box. I sold it a few weeks ago, actually. Those are the only Sampson items I've had for a while, though." He nodded his head as if he was thinking. "I see that's a Sampson ring on your finger. A Pengrath design, if I'm not mistaken." He winked, showing off that he knew his stuff.

After I paid for my purchase, I went back to the truck. I knew who I needed to see if I was going to get the answers I needed about what happened to Prudence. Perception was different from reality in this case, I was sure of it. I was more determined than ever to find out what had happened, and there was one man who I thought held the key to everything.

CHAPTER 15

I climbed in my truck, and tucked Suzy's wedding gift safely in the console. It was getting to be late-afternoon, and I had one more stop to make before I headed over to Billy's for dinner.

I turned off Main Street onto Chestnut and pulled into the parking lot of Snipes Funeral Home. The property was beautifully maintained with the Victorian-era home in which the main building was housed standing, imposing and proper, against the more modest homes that flanked it on either side. I briefly wondered what it must be like living next to a funeral home, and whether the children that grew up next door would tell each other scary stories about the old building.

I walked inside where Mr. Gentry, a gentleman who had worked at the bank when I was a kid, greeted me. *This must be his retirement job. Makes sense – who knows everyone in town better than a banker, and he's certainly accustomed to dealing with people at every stage in life.*

"Hello, how can I help you?" he asked as I walked up to the small desk inside the foyer.

"Hi, Mr. Gentry. You may not remember me – I'm Emma Hooper," I said, realizing that there were many people in town with whom I had grown up but whom I had not yet seen since my return to Hillbilly Hollow months before.

His green eyes brightened with recognition, "Ah, yes, of course! I remember you, Emma. I haven't seen you since, well, I don't remember the last time." He chuckled. "Last I heard you were a city girl now."

I smiled and placed a hand on my chest as if I had been offended.

"Now, Mr. Gentry, you can take the girl out of the country, but you can't take the country out of the girl."

He nodded in agreement, "Ah, then, I apologize, Miss Country Girl. Well, I assume there is no doubt you will be attending Suzy's wedding tomorrow?"

I grinned. "Maid of honor, actually."

He clucked his tongue and placed both hands on top of the small desk. "I should have known. The two of you have been inseparable since you were only kids. I remember when one of you would go missing we would just look for the other. Wherever one of you was, the other was sure to be there as well. Oh, and of course we can't forget Billy, now can we?"

We both laughed light heartedly.

"I remember when you were all just a bunch of kids running around. Now Suzy's saying 'I do'. Time really does fly. Why, it wouldn't surprise me at all if the next wedding was your own," he said with a wink.

"Oh, uh, I'm not too sure I'm ready for that yet, and Billy, well, he's just a friend."

Mr. Gentry smiled. "Well, if you're not ready then I guess that's that, but Emma, he won't wait forever." He winked.

I laughed awkwardly.

Mr. Gentry had always had a kind soul. As I child, I had

looked forward to Grandma's weekly bank visits. I would wake up at the crack of dawn just to ride with her. It had become a sort of weekly adventure. Mr. Gentry had a new story for me to hear every time, and the visits always ended with him handing me a big, red, cherry lollipop.

He was sick once, and an older woman had filled in for him. She was strictly business and at the end of the visit she handed me a mint, of all things. It was a long ride home. I was miserable that day, so when I saw Mr. Gentry the next week back at his usual post I was over the moon.

I felt a small pang of guilt for not coming to see him sooner, and I wondered briefly what other people had yet to learn of my return, but I quickly dismissed the thought. I was on a mission for Prudence. She deserved the truth, and I was running out of time.

"I was hoping to see Mr. Snipes. Is he in today?" My voice displayed far more urgency than I had intended it to.

Mr. Gentry had not seemed to notice, or if he did, he kept it to himself. "He's in his office, but I have to warn you, he has not exactly been much of a conversationalist lately." His voice trailed off, then seeming to remember he was not alone, and there was in fact a customer just a few feet away, he cleared his throat and continued speaking.

"If you have any questions I would be more than happy to help." He must have noticed the worry making its way across my face and misinterpreted it as doubt. "Don't worry, I'm just as knowledgeable as Peter himself, if not more," he finished with a grin.

"Oh, I'm sure you are, Mr. Gentry. I wouldn't expect anything less from you. You've never been one to take a job without learning the inner workings like the back of your hand. I'm just worried about Peter Snipes. Is he okay? I really needed to speak with him today."

It was imperative that I speak to Peter Snipes. He was the

last piece to this puzzle. Who could provide me with more information than Prudence's fiancé himself? If I was going to find out the truth I needed to speak to him.

Mr. Gentry dropped his head, then looked around as if to be sure there were no people close by to hear what he was about to say.

"I'm sure you have heard about Prudence by now. It's such an awful tragedy, and Peter has not been himself since."

I nodded slowly. "So they were close?"

Mr. Gentry lowered his voice. "I'm not one for speculation, but I had never seen Prudence outside of church. Then suddenly she is showing up here daily, bringing Peter lunch, and stopping by for no reason. Peter was just as eager to see her. He would leave his office in the middle of the day, sometimes for hours. And –"

He stopped and ruffled a wrinkly hand through his grey hair. "No, no. I can't say."

I felt bad for Mr. Gentry, he had clearly already said more than he had ever intended to, but it was not enough. If I was going to get to the bottom of this, I needed to know everything. I had to keep pressing.

"Mr. Gentry, please. You can tell me. I won't speak of it to another soul."

He sighed heavily. "All of this occurred while Peter was still seeing Cindy."

My eyes grew wide as the words slipped out of his mouth. I guessed there was some truth to Cindy's speculations after all. Prudence had never struck me as the type to be with a man already spoken for.

If Cindy truly felt that Peter was cheating on her there was no telling the amount of anger and hurt that had caused her. Prudence, of course, would have become the bane of Cindy's existence. Cindy would have blamed her for everything. It sounded an awful lot like motive to me.

Mr. Gentry continued speaking, as I started connecting the dots. "I felt awful answering Cindy's phone calls every day. Telling her Peter was with a client while he was out with Prudence. It had been going on for months. I don't even know where Peter got the time to work, as much time as he was spending with Prudence."

It seemed as though a huge weight had been lifted off of Mr. Gentry's shoulders. I couldn't imagine knowing a secret like that, and having to carry it all on my own. I was in the middle of trying to process all of this when my phone buzzed.

BILLY: Dinner still on?
ME: Yes. Just running some errands.
BILLY: Maid of honor duties?
ME: Yep. What else?
BILLY: Nothing just checking in. Do you want spaghetti or steak?
ME: Doesn't matter

There was a pause, and I shoved my phone back in my pocket. There was too much going on for me to be texting Billy right now. I felt bad for being so short with him, but I was sure he would understand.

That was what made him such a good friend, after all. He was always so understanding and forgiving, no matter the circumstances. Not even five seconds after I had put my phone away, the phone on Mr. Gentry's desk began to ring.

"Snipes Funeral Home. How may I help you?" he answered.

There was a pause.

"Ah, yes. Mrs. Bostic."

I exchanged a strange look with Mr. Gentry when he spoke the name. Mrs. Bostic was such a sweet woman. She would bake cookies for the Sheriff's department every week, and was always looking for ways to help out with the community along with her husband, Todd.

When we were children, she would often make lemonade and pie for Suzy, Billy, and I when we would spend our days outside playing. I wondered why she could be calling the funeral home.

After another long pause, Mr. Gentry spoke again, and I felt my heart break a little. "Yes, ma'am. Todd's cremation will take place first thing tomorrow, and the ashes will be returned to you."

Another stretch of silence.

"Well I'm afraid I don't have too much control over that. It's company policy."

This time the silence was much longer than the others.

"Perhaps we could work something out, but you'll have to talk to Peter about all of that. I'm just the receptionist, after all."

A short pause.

"Be sure to stay in touch, and Betty – if there's ever anything I can do for you don't hesitate to give me a call."

He hung up the phone and sighed. "This work is so much harder when you're in a small town. You know every single client personally."

I nodded my head respectfully. Working with people he knew personally, talking about the process and the financial aspect of it when their loved one had passed just days ago, I imagined that couldn't be easy.

"When did he pass?" I asked quietly.

Mr. Gentry looked up. "Oh, uh, a few nights ago. He went peacefully in his sleep. 78 years is a great, long life, but still, I hate to see Betty so tore up. The worst part is that she can't even afford a proper burial. Cremation was the only other option."

"That's terrible," I said.

Mr. Gentry nodded. "It's far too often the sad reality. Death is something we all face, and of course someone would find a way to make a profit from it. Ours is a booming industry, I'll give it that much. Fads come and go, but dying? That's never going away."

I was surprised to hear this type of opinion coming from a man who worked in a funeral home, of all places. He seemed to notice my change in expression as he shrugged his shoulders.

"What? Just 'cause I don't like profiting from death doesn't mean I can't work here. If you can't beat it then you might as well join it. It's a necessary evil."

We chatted a bit more about the funeral industry and the Bostics. By the time I glanced outside it was beginning to get dark.

"Oh!" I exclaimed, cutting Mr. Gentry's last statement short. "I'm so sorry but I have got to get going! I have a dinner I have to get to."

Mr. Gentry smiled. "No, it's no trouble at all. Sorry to keep you chatting. It was nice catching up with you, Emma."

I said goodbye and quickly made my way outside.

CHAPTER 16

I had nearly reached my truck when I noticed a shape out in the distance behind the funeral home. Upon closer observation, I realized it was Peter Snipes. He was covered in dirt and held a shovel in his hand. Hadn't Mr. Gentry said he was in his office? Why would Peter Snipes let Mr. Gentry think he was in there when he was really outdoors? And what could Snipes possibly be doing outside with a shovel?

I dismissed the first ridiculous thought that his occupation naturally suggested. He might be the director of the funeral home but Snipes was no grave digger and this was no cemetery. Perhaps he was doing a little landscaping around the home.

I began walking towards him, and we reached each other at the halfway point.

"Peter Snipes?" I asked carefully.

His bushy eyebrows twitched in response, and his hand gripped the rod of the shovel.

"Yeah, that's me."

I outstretched my arm and he shook my hand with his

free one. I noticed the dirt caked up under his fingernails and tried my best out of politeness not to wipe my hand off on my pants.

"I'm Emma Hooper, an old friend of Prudence's," I said.

He looked at me blankly for a moment, and then began walking towards the funeral home. It seemed a slightly rude response and I wondered what Prudence had seen in this brusque man.

"She never mentioned an Emma," he called out behind him. It was obvious he was skeptical, and had no interest in talking to me.

I knew I had to do something. This could be my only chance to talk to him before Prudence – Well, before the worst might happen.

I called, "Well, she mentioned you."

He still continued walking, so I knew I had to push harder. "I know about the engagement," I blurted out in a moment of boldness.

That stopped him in his tracks. He turned and faced me.

Making his way closer, he spoke in a hushed tone. "Sh– She told you? We were trying to keep it quiet –"

I cut him off. "Why?"

He looked at me, as if confused.

"Why were you trying to keep it quiet?" I repeated, the accusation loud and clear in my voice.

Peter Snipes sighed and for a moment he looked genuinely distraught. Maybe he wasn't such an unpleasant man after all, at least where Prudence was concerned.

It was only then that I noticed the dark circles under his eyes, and the way his skin seemed to cling to his bones. It was evident he was not getting nearly enough sleep, or food for that matter. This was a man in the deepest depths of loss, grieving for his love, and I was interrogating him and judging him for being brusque.

I felt a pang of guilt for the second time that day. Still, grieving or not, Peter seemed inclined to answer my question. His words were slow, deliberate, almost as if he had said them before.

"With all the talk after Preacher Jacob's death... Prudence was going through a lot. There

were rumors, you know? Everyone acts like they care, but at the end of the day all they care about is what big thing they can gossip about next. We refused to let it be us. With Cindy already tarnishing Prudence's good name, we didn't want anything else to have to deal with. We just wanted to be happy. We were happy..." His voice trailed off and he looked as though he might cry.

He shook his head and cleared his throat. "Well, I thought we were. I don't know why she did what she did. How could I have not seen the signs? She's gone, and I couldn't help her." He put his hand against his head and his shoulders moved up and down as he cried softly.

"She's not gone yet, Peter. You can always have hope. There's always a chance that she could come out of this, and you'll get that wedding you planned on."

He shook his head and mumbled from between his hands, "I lost whatever hope I had when I heard about what she had done to herself."

"Peter, I don't think Prudence tried to take her own life." Maybe I should have kept that to myself, but I couldn't stand to see this man in so much pain, thinking his fiancé tried to take her own life because she wasn't happy. He deserved to know the truth, even if I didn't know the whole truth just yet myself.

"What are you saying right now?"

I breathed in, knowing how much of a shock this must be to him. "I think someone else did this. I believe someone made an attempt on her life."

He shook his head slowly. "No. She took the pills. There was already an investigation."

I disagreed. "Prudence was happier than she has been in a long, long time. If there had been signs, don't you think you would have seen them?"

Again he shook his head sadly. "I wish I could believe you. But Prudence tried to kill herself. She put herself in that coma. There's no use thinking any different. Goodbye, Miss Hooper."

He headed off into the funeral home without another word.

I wondered if I should go after him to apologize for the comments that had obviously only troubled him further, but the darkening sky told me that if I didn't leave at that moment I would be late for dinner. I rushed over to my truck and made my way to Billy's.

My mind was racing the whole ride there. So Prudence really had been seeing Peter while he was still with Cindy. That gave Cindy more motive than anyone else. Still, would she really go as far as to try and kill Prudence? All over Peter? It seemed to be the only explanation, but I still could not quite figure Peter Snipes out.

Why would he cheat on Cindy, instead of just ending the relationship? Why hadn't he believed me when I suggested Prudence hadn't done this to herself? No, Cindy might have the most motive, but there was also something about Peter Snipes that didn't add up.

CHAPTER 17

I arrived at Billy's house, more than fashionably late, and hurried to the door. I knocked only twice before the door swung open and I was greeted by Billy wearing a huge grin. "I was beginning to think you weren't going to make it."

I made my way inside and was greeted by a delicious smell. "And miss out on your spectacular cooking? No way," I teased. Billy had a natural gift for cooking. When we were younger he was always coming up with new food inventions. Most of them were completely inedible, like the time he invented a ketchup and strawberry jam sandwich, but when he did something right, it was absolutely delectable.

He used to dream of being a chef, but in the end he decided cooking was not enough. He wanted to do something selfless, to dedicate his life to serving others. It was a surprise to most people when he pursued a career in the medical field, but not to me. I knew Billy better than anyone, and his career choice just made sense. It was just who he was, who he had always been.

He led me to the wooden table in his dining room and

pulled out a chair. The table was set with beautiful china adorned with small green vines painted along the edges of the plates and cups. The silverware wore a similar vine engraving on the handles of each piece of cutlery. It was clear that these beautiful pieces of dining ware had not been used in quite some time.

I looked around and took a moment to admire all the beautiful photography hanging around the room. One photo was of a rain puddle, a leaf floating gently along. Another featured a child sitting on a bench, her mother squatting down in front of her tying her shoe laces. The one that stuck out the most, however, was of an old man sitting on a corner, face turned up to the sky, eyes closed as if he was praying.

"These photos are amazing." I looked at Billy. "Mind sharing the name of the photographer with me? I'd love to get a few of their pieces of my own."

Billy smiled. "Well, I'm sure I could get you some of their photos no problem. I'm the one who took them, after all."

I shook my head in disbelief. "Really? You took these?"

He nodded. "Yep. I was pretty big into photography in high school, remember?"

Of course I remembered. He had made life miserable for me and Suzy for nearly two months, following us around, taking photos at any given opportunity. I chuckled at the memory, "Well yeah, but these are exquisite!"

I tore my attention away from the photos and locked eyes with Billy, who was grinning even bigger than he had when I'd first arrived. I glanced away. In the middle of the table was a vase with a single rose, and a candle flickered dimly next to it. I couldn't help but feel that perhaps Billy saw this evening as something other than what it was. Before the thought had any more time to sink in, Billy made his way to the kitchen and walked out a few moments later with a huge bowl in one hand and a stack of plates and small bowls in the other.

He set down the biggest bowl and I saw it was filled to the brim with spaghetti. He brought out a plate with two plump, perfectly cooked steaks, a bowl full of mashed potatoes, and another bowl of salad.

"What is all of this?" I asked, mouth gaping in awe of the large amount of food for only two people.

"Well," he said as he made his way back into the kitchen, "I asked if you wanted steak or spaghetti, and you didn't give me a straight answer." He came back out with a bottle of wine. "So we're having both," he finished with a charming smile.

I laughed and felt the tops of my cheek getting flushed. "Billy, you have really outdone yourself."

He smirked. "I'm not too sure if I can agree with that. I think I'll be eating spaghetti leftovers for a while – and I don't even like spaghetti." This sent both of us into a fit of laughter.

The night was spent reminiscing over old memories, drinking, laughing, and eating until we were both too full to take another bite.

"Oh man, I am going to be so bloated I might not even fit into my dress tomorrow."

Billy chuckled. "I don't think Suzy would be too happy about that. Can you just imagine her reaction?"

I laughed so hard I nearly spit out my drink. "She would have a break down! She has worked so hard to get everything perfect for this wedding, but still her face would be priceless."

Billy raised an eyebrow. "Well, if you want to see that face so badly, then who am I to stop you?" He got up and walked into the kitchen. I wondered what he was doing. Moments later, he emerged holding a chocolate cake with both hands.

"What? You made cake too? Billy, I can *not* eat that."

He set it down and began cutting a slice. "Not even one slice?"

The smell was tantalizing, but I knew I had to resist. "I'm the maid of honor. I have a duty to the bride, and part of that duty is making sure I can fit into my dress on her big day!"

Billy chuckled and threw his hands up in mock defeat. "Alright, alright. You've got me there."

We sat in comfortable quietness for a moment before Billy broke the silence. "She finally made it."

The sound of his voice snapped me out of my wondering thoughts of Prudence and all the questions I still had. "Hmm?" I asked.

"Suzy. She has come a long way. It feels like only yesterday we were a couple of kids getting ourselves into trouble. I can't believe she's getting married tomorrow. Don't get me wrong, Brian is a great guy. It's just, well, we will never really be the Three Musketeers again." He looked down at his hands and took a sip of his drink.

"Maybe not," I began, "but if Suzy loves Brian, then I love him too. We might not ever be the Three Musketeers again, but who says we can't be the Fabulous Four?"

Billy chuckled. "Always the optimist, Emma. You would not be yourself if you weren't." He leaned back in his chair. "I like the Fabulous Four. It has a nice ring to it."

I sipped on my drink. "Not as nice as the Three Muske-teers, but it works."

Billy set his glass down and looked at me seriously. "Emma, are you okay? You've seemed so distracted all night. Like your mind is anywhere but here."

There were so many things I wanted to tell him. I wouldn't even know where to start. But I knew that I couldn't tell, no matter how much I wanted to. It's not exactly easy to explain that the spirit of a woman in a coma visited you, and now you're having a hard time figuring out the truth. Of course, he already knew that I sometimes saw ghosts since my accident. But to him it was a scientific phenomenon with a medical explanation. Just misfiring synapses in my brain. He didn't know how real the ghosts had become to me, or that I felt compelled to investigate their fates. That was too crazy for me to say aloud, even to Billy.

So instead I smiled and said, "Oh, well, to be honest with you, Billy, I'm just a little nervous about tomorrow. I mean there's so many things that have to go right. I guess I'm also just a little nervous for Suzy. I want everything to go perfectly for her."

Billy nodded in agreement. "I understand. I feel the same way. Suzy has worked so hard on all of this. We both know how she can be sometimes. That's why I'm trying my best not to worry. If anyone could pull off an event as big as this, it's Suzy."

"I still can't really believe tomorrow is finally the day. I'm going to be a crying mess."

Billy shuffled in his chair. "Speaking of tomorrow, I know you will be busy during the ceremony doing your maid of honor duties, but I was thinking if it's not too much to ask then during the reception, well, maybe –"

"OH. MY. GOSH!" I cut him off. "Is it really already 10:30?"

Billy looked forlorn as I got up and began grabbing my things. I didn't really mind the time, but I had a feeling I knew where this conversation was going, and wasn't looking forward to it. I made my way to the door.

CHAPTER 18

"*L*et me walk you out," Billy offered.

"Oh no, it's fine. I had a great time. The food was delicious!"

Billy started to say something, but I quickly made my way to the truck. I turned back to see him watching me from the doorway for a moment more before slowly closing the door.

I breathed a huge sigh of relief. *What is it with this town?* It seemed like no matter where I went the pressure was on for me to be with Billy. I cared about Billy, he meant more to me than probably anyone else, and that was exactly why I could never be with him. Why couldn't anyone else see that?

Our friendship, our childhood, all of our memories... It was all so precious to me. None of it was worth throwing away. I couldn't take that risk, no matter how badly anyone else wanted me to. No matter how badly even I wanted to.

Anyway, this wasn't the time to be thinking about possible love interests. Tomorrow was the wedding and I still didn't have a single clue as to what had happened to Prudence. As I began driving home, I had a bad feeling I couldn't shake off. I pulled up to my grandparents' home, and gently took the keys out of the ignition.

I crept in quietly, and made my way up to the attic as silently as possible. My grandparents were already asleep by now and there was no reason to wake them. Snowball was already sleeping next to my bed when I finally made my way inside. The little goat stirred and bleated softly when I sat on the bed.

"Shh. Go back to sleep, Snowball," I cooed quietly. The goat only bleated again. I pushed myself off of the bed and onto the floor next to Snowball. I ran my hand gently along the smooth fur on Snowball's back. "What am I going to do, Snowball? The wedding is tomorrow and I don't feel one step closer to figuring this all out than I did when Prudence first came to me." The goat curled up next to me and drifted off to sleep.

I crept back onto my bed and I threw my head back, staring at the ceiling. I felt a pit of sadness deep in my stomach. "I'm sorry Prudence," I whispered quietly. "I am so sorry." I had visited everyone I could think of, asked every question I had, and still I was no closer to the truth than I was before. I had let Prudence down.

Just as sleep was beginning to creep up on me, making my eyelids feel so very heavy, I had an overwhelming urge to grab Prudence's Diary. I frantically flipped through the pages until I landed on the one I was searching for.

P.S - CHECK STATE RECORDS. History? License? CANNOT BE TRUE!

P.S. WHY DID that sound so familiar? *P.S.* I flipped back through the diary to the first Saturday of September. *P.S.* in blue ink with the little red heart just as I had remembered it. Of course! How could I have been so blind?

I was so caught up in the feud with Ambrose Snodgrass, that I had forgotten that P.S could be initials. *Peter Snipes!* But why did Prudence feel the need to check state records on Peter Snipes? What could she mean by 'cannot be true'?

I reread the short sentence. I never knew one sentence could be so important, could hold all the answers to such a huge question. When she mentioned the license, was Prudence possibly talking about Peter's mortician license? What made her question everything? As my own questions grew larger, so did the implications they held.

I pulled out my laptop and searched Peter Snipes again. I recalled he had been a mortician at a larger chain in Kansas City. I found the name, then did a quick search. I had assumed he had simply left the business, so I was surprised to see he had actually been terminated.

I tried to find the specific details, but the only comment that had been made about his termination was, "unethical practices". I wondered what could have led Prudence to needing to find this information out, and what practices could Peter have been performing.

The sound of my phone ringing nearly made me leap out of my skin. I glanced at it to see that Suzy was giving me a call. *Why is she up so late the night before her wedding?*

I picked up right away.

"Hello?" I answered tentatively.

"Hey, Emma." Her voice was tired.

"What's going on?" I asked.

"Huh? Oh, nothing really. I mean, nothing at all, actually. I just can't sleep. I've got nervous jitters."

"Of course you do. You're marrying the man of your dreams tomorrow!"

I heard Suzy let out a small giggle.

"I feel like a kid on Christmas Eve again. You remember how much fun we used to have together on Christmas Eve?"

"Of course, it was one of my favorite times every year," I said cheerfully.

We would stay up at Suzy's house, Billy and I, drinking hot chocolate, watching Christmas specials, and trying to guess which gifts each of us would receive the following morning. Our guesses were never right. We would end up saying things we hoped for, rather than what we really got.

Although Suzy had been adamant one year that she would receive a car. Her enthusiasm was so contagious that I would have believed it too, if only Billy hadn't been such a skeptic.

"I miss that." Suzy's voice seemed full of nostalgia.

"I do too. We're all grown up now. Suzy, it's getting pretty late. Don't you think you should try and get some rest?"

She sighed. "Yeah, I guess you're right. Thanks for chatting with me. See you tomorrow!"

With that, the phone clicked to silence. I held it in my hand for a moment longer.

Suddenly, a loud noise echoed up through the house. It sounded like the back door slamming. I jumped up and quickly made my way downstairs. I ran outside to see Grandma in her nightgown crossing the lawn toward the chicken coop. She stopped just a little distance short of the coop and I caught up to her. I gently touched her arm.

"Grandma, what's going on this time?"

She looked at me with glassy eyes. "It's Nancy. She's starting an argument with Pat tonight!"

I took her elbow and slowly led her back toward the house.

"Wow! Pat is just up to all kinds of drama lately. First Dolley, now Nancy. I wonder what has gotten into her."

Grandma made a small pfft sound and pointed a finger.

"She's tired of being bossed around, that's what. Serves 'em right if you ask me."

I couldn't help but chuckle as we met Grandpa at the back door.

He grabbed her hand and spoke to her softly. "Come on, Dorothy. We've got a wedding to attend tomorrow and you wouldn't want to be too tired for that." He looked at me. "Same goes for you, Emma. I'll take her from here."

I smiled and made my way back to the attic. Grandpa had always loved Grandma so much. He treated her with such kindness and tenderness, even during her funny spells. I could only pray I would find a love like that one day.

As I cuddled into my blankets, the events of the day played over and over in my mind. I was still not sure what had happened to Prudence but the pieces were beginning to fall together. I thought of Suzy, and how gorgeous she would look tomorrow on her big day. I thought of Mr. Gentry and how nice it was to catch up. I thought of Peter Snipes and wondered for a moment if he could have been the attempted murderer, or if it was Cindy or Ambrose. I played this question in my mind a few times as I drifted off to sleep.

CHAPTER 19

The next thing I knew, my grandma was gently stirring me awake. I couldn't even remember falling asleep.

"Good morning, Emma. Today is the big day," she said with bright eyes and a smile on her face.

I sat up with a yawn, stretching my arms out behind my head. "Guess it's show time," I giggled groggily.

All throughout breakfast I felt giddy. It wasn't even my wedding day, but I still felt like a happy teenager. Grandma had really outdone herself. Fried eggs, big, fluffy pancakes, and grits to top it all off. It was delicious and my spirits were high.

"Oh, Ed, don't you just love weddings?" Grandma's voice was sickly sweet, and she had both hands propped up on the table, holding her chin.

Grandpa only nodded in response, too busy shoveling grits into his mouth.

"Ah, it reminds me of when we were young and in love," she continued.

I smiled at the fondness in Grandma's face. "How did Grandpa propose to you, Grandma?"

She grinned. "Now that is an interesting story…" She seemed to be recalling the events, as if she didn't want to skip a single detail.

"It was an unusually warm October day. I remember because we were on our way to have a wonderful little picnic in the park. I was carrying the basket and Ed had the blanket wrapped up in his arms. We talked about our dreams and goals on the walk down to the picnic area. The sun was shining, birds were singing, and the breeze was so gentle that even the leaves on the trees were completely still. When we reached the picnic area I dug around in the basket for the lemonade while Ed laid out the blanket. When I turned around, he was kneeling on one knee, holding a blade of grass he'd tied together into a ring, and he asked me to be his wife."

I giggled. "A blade of grass?"

Grandma nodded and laughed. "Yep! He didn't want to waste money on a ring that would eventually never fit anyways. Besides, as he said, it's not the ring that matters but rather the love we share together."

I looked over to see Grandpa nodding slowly, a tiny smile on his lips.

Suddenly, my phone buzzed. It was a text from Suzy.

SUZY: Where r u? I need my maid of honor
ME: Eating breakfast. Whats up?
SUZY: Bridal emergency. Need u.
ME: On my way

"I've got to go. Suzy needs me," I said as I hugged Grandma.

"Oh, go on ahead then. Calm her down, and remind her

what this is all about. I know the feeling of cold feet all too well," she said with a laugh.

"Thanks, Grandma," I said.

I grabbed my things and ran outside to my truck. It suddenly dawned on me that I didn't have a clue where Suzy was. I pulled out my phone and sent her a quick text.

ME: Where r u?
SUZY: At church
ME: Already? 4 hours until show time
SUZY: I was nervous. Needed to make sure everything was being handled

That was just like Suzy. While most brides would love to sleep in and let the wedding party do all the setting up, Suzy had to be sure everything was going according to plan. I smiled to myself.

ME: Ok. Be there soon
SUZY: Hurry pls

CHAPTER 20

I got to the venue as quickly as I could. The church was breathtakingly beautiful. The grass outside was freshly mowed and people were already beginning to show up for the final preparations. Small herds of workers were scurrying around adding the final decor touches. It was coming along unbelievably quickly. The ceremony was not for another three hours, but everything seemed so put together already.

I scurried inside, stopping a woman holding a small decorative flower in her hands.

"Excuse me, do you know where the bride is?" I asked.

The young woman's blue eyes stood out sharply against her pale skin. Her bright pink lips pulled into a small frown. "She's in the back. Bless her heart, she's having a meltdown." She shook her head. "Nothing like cold feet on the day of the wedding."

I thanked the woman for her time, then made my way towards the back. Suzy was sitting on a small love seat in her dressing room, head resting between both hands.

I gently placed my hand on her back. "Maid of honor reporting for duty."

She looked up and her cheeks were bright red and tear-stained. "Oh, Emma!" she exclaimed as she wrapped her arms around me. "I think I have made a mistake."

I pulled back from her. "What are you talking about, Suz?"

She wiped her arm across her face, drying the tears just in time for them to be replaced by fresh, new ones. "How do I know he's the one?" she asked. "How can I guarantee I want to spend the rest of my life with him?"

I had heard of people catching cold feet before, but this seemed so shockingly unexpected. "Suzy, this is Brian we're talking about. The same Brian that you, the bossiest person I know, let take control of your honeymoon plans. You wouldn't allow just anyone to do something like that."

Suzy sniffled and placed a hand on mine. "Yes I know, but it's just such a huge commitment, and with all the excitement and giddiness and wedding planning, I guess it never really had time to sink in until now."

I wrapped my fingers around her hand. "Suzy. You remember what you told me the other night when I walked in on your, er, meditation?"

She giggled at the memory. "You were so scared." She sighed. "I don't remember what I said, Emma."

I looked into her eyes seriously. "You said it's all about marrying Brian. It's about the two of you standing up and saying you want to be together forever, and when you said those words I know you meant it, Suzy. I have never seen you wear a bigger smile than in that moment, but I know you will be wearing an even bigger smile today when you finally say those vows."

Suzy's eyes were filling with tears once more, and for a moment I feared I had only made things worse. Then she wrapped me up in another hug and laughed. "I don't know what I would do without you. You are the greatest friend I have, and I would be lost without you."

Now it was my turn to tear up. "You're my best friend in the whole entire world, Suzy. I will always be here for you." We hugged for a few more moments, then Suzy wiped her face once more and jumped to her feet.

She clapped her hands together three times. "Now, chop chop. We have a wedding to tackle, and you, my dear maid of honor, need to get your makeup done. You look completely exhausted. I mean, seriously, did you wrestle a hen last night?"

I laughed. "Uh, something like that."

The next couple of hours were a blur. From makeup, hair, and everything in between I felt like I was spinning my wheels.

Later, I was sitting on the small loveseat catching my breath when Suzy came running into the room.

"It's ruined!" she exclaimed with a small stomp of her foot. "I can't believe it!"

I stood up and decidedly ignored Suzy's small bridezilla moment. After all, this was her big day and she deserved everything to be perfect. "Suzy, look at me. Breathe," I said.

She stared at me and nodded her head as she grabbed my hands.

"Now tell me, what happened?"

She breathed in, then let the words fall out in a frenzied mess. "Everything was perfect, but now the whole thing is ruined! The photographer can't make it, says he is sick – the flu or something. If he thinks he's keeping the deposit, he is so wrong. I can't believe this. Seriously, on the day of my wedding? I don't even have time to find a replacement now. This is a disaster!"

I nodded my head. "Well, to be fair, it's not like he can

choose whether or not he gets sick. I'm sure he's just as disappointed as you are, but I agree this is a disaster." I glanced down at my phone. There was still one hour left until the ceremony. "But I think I might have a solution."

Suzy raised an eyebrow. "Oh really?"

I smiled as I opened my messaging app. "I have a few tricks up my sleeve."

ME: Hey. U said i could get some of those pics anytime right?
BILLY: I'll have to talk to the photographer but i think i can work something out
ME: I dont want the pics. Want the photographer.
BILLY: Huh?
ME: Long story. Suzys photographer is a no show. Need a new one
BILLY: On my way.
ME: Thx billy

I added a smiley face to the end of the message and put my phone back in my pocket. I looked up at Suzy with smile. "It's all taken care of."

She seemed skeptical. "What did you do?"

I grinned from ear to ear. "You remember that old camera Billy used to play around with?"

"Yeah, how could I forget? He practically terrorized us with that thing," she said with a laugh.

I said, "Turns out he still uses it. When we had dinner last night I saw some of the photos he took. I think he has real talent. He will bring his camera and take pictures of the ceremony, and the best part? You will get a free photographer. That's if you don't mind losing him as an usher. I figured photographer was a more important role."

Suzy grinned. "Emma, you are such a life saver!"

"Well, you didn't just make me your maid of honor for no reason," I teased.

"What would I do without you?" Suzy asked as she hugged me again. "I'm so sorry for being such an emotional roller coaster today."

I pulled back. "Hey, it's your wedding day. I think you're allowed to have a few break downs. In fact, I think it's actually kind of expected."

"Thank you, Emma. Also, I hope you know you're not off the hook just because it's my wedding day. Later I wanna hear all about this 'dinner' you two had last night!"

We both laughed, then Suzy gave my hand a squeeze before she rushed off to finish a few more minor details before the ceremony.

CHAPTER 21

The next hour was a blur. Billy showed up and tapped my shoulder while I was sipping from the water fountain inside the church. I turned to him and smiled. His hair was slicked back and he was wearing a nice tan suit with a tan vest to match. He looked so handsome, I glanced away awkwardly.

"Wow, Emma. You look amazing. I guess all that talk about being bloated last night was just that. Talk."

I smiled nervously. "Well, if I would have taken you up on that slice of cake you might not be saying that."

He grinned. "Hey, so about last night, what I was trying to ask you was –"

"Billy! I have never been more happy to see you in my whole entire life than I am in this moment." Suzy came running up to him and gave him a quick hug.

"Wow. Suzy, I am at a loss for words. You look so –"

She cut him off and did a little twirl. "Beautiful? Amazing? Perfect?"

Billy laughed. "All of that and more."

Suzy smiled, then revealed a small piece of paper with a string attached from behind her back.

"This," she said as she hung the string around Billy's neck, "is for you."

The paper read PHOTOGRAPHER in big, bold letters.

"I don't want any confusion on who is the photographer, I mean honestly, I should not have to explain to Aunt Deirdre that just because she owns a phone with a camera application, it does *not* make her a photographer."

Me and Billy exchanged a look. This was so typical of Suzy, being her usual bossy self. It put a smile on both of our faces.

"Yes, captain," Billy responded jokingly.

Suzy rolled her eyes. "That is yes *bride* to you. Today is my wedding, after all. Now come on! We have to take pictures of the wedding party." She turned to me. "And that includes you, Emma."

The wedding party pictures were hectic and a bit crazy. I felt bad for Billy being run around so much by Suzy, but I had to admit it was slightly entertaining. Everything went by so quickly, and before I knew it, it was nearly time for the ceremony to begin.

I was watching the herd of people slowly calm, when I felt a gentle tap on my shoulder. I turned to see Mrs. Bostic smiling at me. Her brown eyes looked even darker with the circles she was sporting underneath them. She was normally a plump woman, but it appeared as though she had lost a few pounds since Todd's passing.

She said, "When Gentry told me you were in town I just couldn't believe I hadn't seen you for myself yet! You sure know how to hide, Emma."

I found myself feeling guilty yet again. "I guess I have been a little busy. I'm sorry for not seeing you earlier. I was sorry to hear about Todd. He was a great man."

"Oh, don't flatter him too much. He always did let things go to his head. If you had said decent, or even good, I might have believed you, but great? That's a stretch." She let out a laugh that didn't even sound halfway real.

I said, "Well, to a couple of kids who were always given lemonade and cookies, I'd say he was pretty great."

She smiled and grabbed my hand gently. "You bunch have grown up so quickly. Enjoy it. Sometimes life passes you by so fast you don't have time to notice it." She pulled me a little closer and leaned in to add, "I better get an invitation to the next wedding as well." She tapped my shoulder and laughed. "Don't worry, I'm only joking."

As the guests were filing in, one in particular caught my attention: Peter Snipes. He was wearing a nice button up shirt, and despite his sad expression, he actually looked quite nice.

I approached him cautiously. "Peter," I said as I gently tapped his shoulder.

He turned and smiled vaguely once he saw me, a stark contrast to the brusque man whom I had just spoken to last night.

"Emma Hooper, right?" he asked, pointing at me.

As he pointed, I noticed small flecks that looked like ashes falling from his coat. He must have noticed me staring, because he wiped the rest of the ashes away quickly. "Sorry about that. I was burning some old papers earlier and I guess I didn't do a very good job cleaning up."

"Oh, don't worry about it," I said dismissively.

Peter put his hands by his sides, fingers grasping at his pant legs nervously. "I want to apologize if I was curt with you the other night. I realize now that you were only trying to help. As I'm sure you can imagine, I've been pretty torn up over Prudence's, um, situation. It hasn't been easy. I have reached out to her mother, sent her flowers, but nothing really eases the ache, I'm afraid sometimes I get a bit –"

"You sent flowers?" I questioned, already knowing the answer.

"Yes, I sent the best arrangement I could find." Then he muttered more quietly under his breath, "And certainly the most expensive."

I smiled reassuringly. "No reason to apologize. Especially not on a wonderful day like this. I'll see you around, Peter."

I began to walk away, then glanced back over my shoulder to see him still watching me.

Peter was wealthy, that much I knew, and it was his wealth that had deceived him in the end. I had seen the beautiful arrangement he had sent Prudence, but what Peter did not know, was that I had also seen the note that came with the flowers. Just two short words, 'I'm Sorry', but with more context now those two words had told me everything I needed to know.

CHAPTER 22

I had no doubt Peter had tried to murder Prudence, but one question was shouting loudly in my head: why? My thoughts were interrupted as Billy grabbed my arm.

"Emma, the ceremony is starting in twenty minutes. You have to go get in your spot–" He stopped short when he saw the look on my face. "Is everything okay?"

I feigned a smile. "Of course. Just nerves, I guess."

I could tell by the look on his face that he wasn't buying it, but we didn't have time to discuss it. He nodded quickly, then made his way to his position.

I rushed inside and found Suzy. She locked eyes with me and she looked as though she might vomit.

"Here we go," I said softly.

"I think I'm going to be sick," Suzy said with a sigh.

"You've got this. Once you see Brian all your fears will melt away."

Suzy nodded her head. "Gosh, I sure hope so."

I stood in my spot twirling both of my thumbs nervously, although admittedly, I didn't know what I was more nervous about, my part in the wedding ceremony, or the fact that Peter Snipes was in the crowd of guests.

I jumped when I heard the processional music begin. It was a mixture of a piano and a beautiful violin. I smiled as I realized it was a gorgeous rendition of *Amazing Grace*. Such a timeless piece. Only Suzy would be able to choose a song that kept things modern, while adding a touch of class to her ceremony.

The line seemed to move so slowly, as though the family members and groomsmen were taking their precious time. I knew it was probably only a matter of minutes, but the nervous anxiety that was tugging at my stomach made me feel impatient. All too soon, the bridesmaids began to make their way out and I wished for a moment that the line would have taken only a bit longer.

I fought back my nervousness and reminded myself I had to be strong. Not only for Suzy, but for Prudence. As my turn to walk came, I held my head high out of respect for the two women I was walking for.

The guests were smiling brightly, and I caught my grandma giving me a small wave. I smiled cheerfully in her direction, then looked around the crowd once more. Billy was taking pictures, and I wasn't the only one who noticed that his focus seemed to have shifted towards me. Snap after snap he kept the camera aimed on me. I felt myself blushing as I made eye contact with him.

I widened my eyes and looked around me as if to say, "There are other people here too, you know." Now it was his turn to blush, and he swiftly turned the camera towards the groom, snapping a few uninspired pictures. Only then did I catch sight of Peter Snipes, looking thoughtfully in my direction. Was he wondering what I might know? What I might guess?

Our eyes met across the distance and it was at that

moment that we both somehow gained a mutual understanding. A shiver passed through me, under his cold gaze. I
knew what he had done, and more importantly, he knew that
I knew. Any doubt I may have had vanished, and it was all
suddenly clear. The fake tears, the flowers, everything. All
signs of a guilty conscience.

I wanted to stop the wedding, to tell everyone the truth,
but I had no proof. I had no evidence, not even as much as a
motive. Besides that, this was the day Suzy had dreamed
about since she was a little girl. I could never forgive myself
if I ruined this for her. So instead, I bit my tongue and
clenched my shaking hands around the flowers I carried.

As I finally made my way to the front of the church and
stood in my spot, the music faded out and was replaced with
a new song. The ultimate classic, *Here Comes the Bride*, and
how suiting it was. As everyone stood to watch Suzy enter, I
thought every heart surely stopped for a moment.

She was so gorgeous. I had expected tears, but not so
early on. Still, I found myself wiping my eyes every few
seconds. It was useless as the tears just kept flooding my face.
Suzy's eyes were locked on Brian's, and as I glanced over at
him, I noticed he was in the same predicament I was in.

Suzy seemed to move in slow motion. Every step was
beautiful. She was full of grace, and I was so proud of the
woman she had become. As she reached the front the music
slowly ended, and she shot me a quick smile.

From where I was standing I heard the officiant clear his
throat, then speak. "Dearly beloved, we are gathered here
today to witness the marriage of Brian and Suzy. They have
chosen to spend their lives together, and they have invited
you, friends and family, to join them on the greatest day of
their lives.

Love is something we all search for, and they have found
it in each other. Marriage is a commitment to choose to

continue to grow that love every single day. It is a small sapling that with enough sunlight and water, will grow into a beautiful Oak tree one day. So long as they nurture and care for their marriage, they will see the fruits of their labor.

Their love will be as strong and unyielding as the tall Oak. This will not be an easy journey, but it is the greatest journey you will take in both of your lives."

As the officiant shuffled his papers around, I noticed everyone was a bit teary eyed. Everyone except Peter Snipes.

P.S - check state records. History? License? CANNOT BE TRUE!

The entry from Prudence's diary was repeating itself in my head. She knew something. Whatever 'unethical practices' Peter had been terminated for, he hadn't stopped in Kansas City. He'd continued them here. Prudence found out, and with a business as well off as his I was sure he would have done anything to save it. Even if that meant killing his fiancé.

"These vows you are about to make are an eternal promise to one another. They are the guide by which you must base your marriage on." The speaker turned towards the groom.

"Brian, do you take Suzy to be your lawfully wedded wife, to have and to hold, from this day forward, for better and for worse, for richer and poorer, in sickness and in health, till death do you part?"

Brian smiled as Suzy wiped a tear from her eye. "I do," he said confidently.

The officiant turned towards Suzy. "Suzy, do you take Brian to be your lawfully wedded husband, to have and to hold, from this day forward, for better and for worse, for richer and poorer, in sickness and in health, till death do you part?"

"Yes! I mean, I do." Suzy giggled as Brian tried to hold in

his laughter. The officiant grinned and it wasn't long before the whole crowd was laughing. Suzy was almost in tears from laughing so hard. I had never seen her as happy as she was in this moment.

As the laughter quieted down the officiant cleared his throat once more. "Do you have the rings?"

I stepped forward, along with the best man, and we provided the rings we'd been carrying. Suzy reached for hers and flashed me a huge grin.

"Let these rings be a statement of your never ending love for one another. Just as this ring has no end, neither shall your love for each other end."

They slipped the rings on one another's fingers softly and then turned back to the officiant.

"It is my great honor to pronounce you husband and wife. You may now kiss your bride."

Brian leaned in gently, but it was Suzy who stole the show. She grabbed his face with both of her hands and planted a passionate kiss on his lips.

The guests "ooed" and clapped. Soon the whole church broke out in a roar of cheering as the bride and groom hurried off down the aisle.

As the crowd began to rush out after them, eager to get to the reception, I desperately wanted to go with them all, but from the corner of my eye I saw Peter sneaking out of the church.

CHAPTER 23

I made my exit quietly and followed Peter Snipes. I wondered where he could be going. Surely he knew by now that I was following him. Wasn't that why he had slipped out, after all? He wanted to speak to me. Alone, no doubt.

It didn't take me long to realize he was going towards the oldest part of the church, the bell house. I grew worried, but still I followed. I entered the shadowed, lonely space to see a spiraling staircase up ahead. Peter was already nearly halfway up the steps.

I breathed in deeply and gathered my courage. As I climbed each step, a sense of dread was finding its way deep within me. It took everything I had not to just turn back. But I couldn't leave without forcing answers from him. Prudence was counting on me. Prudence, who was barely clinging to life and might not have much time left. In the face of that horrible ticking clock, doing the sensible thing and going looking for Billy or someone else to back me up wasn't an option. Besides, Peter surely wouldn't talk in front of anyone else. Something told me he would talk to me, though.

As I finally reached the top of the stairs, I saw Peter standing there, waiting, with his back to me.

"How did you find out?" His voice was completely blank, devoid of any and all feeling. If he held any emotion he didn't show it, and somehow that made everything more sinister.

Cautiously, I kept my distance. "I think the more pressing question is why did you do it?"

He shrugged, and I felt chills run up and down my spine at the casual response. Or maybe the chills were from the wind, which seemed strong up here in the top of the tower, where the open sides gave sweeping views of the surrounding countryside.

Peter Snipes spoke, distracting me from the sight of the emptying parking lot far below. He said, "Why does the lion hunt? Why does a cornered dog attack? It's called survival, and it's pure instinct."

He finally turned to face me, and I realized rather quickly why his voice held no emotion. The emotion was written all across his features and it was ugly. Harsh.

"It's instinct to try and kill someone who loved you as much as Prudence did?" I demanded.

"I loved her too," he spat back.

He must have seen my disbelief.

"I did," he said through clenched teeth. "I loved her more than anyone I've ever known. I wanted to marry her, to spend our lives together. When she first got suspicious, I begged her to just let it go, but she wouldn't stop. She kept digging, kept investigating. She was always so smart…"

His voice trailed off as if he were talking about just anyone and not some woman he had attempted to murder. Then he went on, "She figured out the truth, and it still wasn't enough. She wanted to tell everyone, and I couldn't let that happen. She threw away our future and all for what? A few bodies that were dumped into shallow, shared graves instead of a proper burial or cremation? Who cares?"

So that was what his 'unethical practices' had been. He'd been cutting corners in a gruesome way to keep down his business's costs. I thought back to the other night when I had confronted him. He had been holding a shovel. *He had just finished dumping a body! No wonder he acted so strangely then.*

He started to step towards me now and I cautiously took a step back.

Stalling for time, I said, "Yesterday you buried Todd Bostic in one of your secret mass graves, didn't you? But Mrs. Bostic was supposed to pick up the ashes today. What did you give her instead?"

He continued to move towards me, and I continued to edge away, just barely aware of the fact that we were circling each other.

He answered, "The usual. I give them burnt scraps of paper or whatever I have around at the moment."

He took another step forward. I stepped back again.

"Cutting corners at the funeral home? That's what this was all about? You were willing to kill someone you claim to love over a career?" I asked.

He laughed, a sudden, wild sound that seemed out of place in the silence of the bell tower. "A career? This is my family's legacy! I couldn't let her ruin it, and she knew that."

He took another step towards me. I went to take a step back and noticed the dwindling space between me and the open drop off from the bell tower. Only a very low and flimsy railing stood between me and a fall of nearly thirty feet.

Even in my precarious position, I couldn't hide my disgust at what he had done to Prudence. "You talk about your family's legacy?" I asked. "I think you ruined that all on your own the moment you started lying to your grieving patients!"

"My patients are always satisfied. It's not the body they seek, it's the comfort. Who cares what's in the urn so long as it provides them with some peace?" He ran a hand through his hair. "Anyway, now that you know the truth I can't afford to let you spill it."

He reached out towards me, grabbing my wrist. I pulled back but his grip was too tight. He jerked me around and I stumbled, only to land on the floor. I felt the breath whoosh from my lungs at the impact. His other hand reached towards my throat, but before it had time to connect, I bit the hand that was still clutching my wrist. He screamed and released his grip on me.

I glanced behind me to see that I was just inches away from the edge of the bell platform, and Peter was already approaching me again. His eyes were wild and I knew he had every intention of killing me.

"Peter, you don't have to do this," I pleaded.

"You see that's where you're wrong. If I let you live, you'll tell everyone what I did to Prudence, the same way she was going to tell everyone about the funeral home."

As he stepped closer, I looked down at the fall below me, my palms growing sweaty. Surviving a fall like that didn't seem likely.

CHAPTER 24

*A*s I was weighing my options I saw a small movement out of the corner of my eye.

I couldn't believe it. Standing at the top of the staircase behind Peter, eyes bulging at the surprising scene before him, was Tucker. He looked confused, but more than anything concerned. Even Tucker could surely see that if I made one wrong move, my life could be over in a matter of seconds. I saw his hand move as if reaching for his gun, but then stop as he undoubtedly realized that he wasn't carrying a weapon, not at a wedding.

Peter seemed unaware of Tucker's presence, and I subtly shook my head, warning the sheriff to keep back.

"Peter, I won't tell anyone," I said, trying to distract my attacker. "Your secret is safe with me."

Peter sighed. "That's exactly what Prudence said that last night we had dinner together, but I couldn't take the chance of trusting her. It was almost too easy, really, once I accepted what had to be done. I ordered strong pills from an online pharmacy. Then I invited myself over for dinner that night and insisted on preparing the food alone. I crushed the pills

– a deadly amount of them – and slipped them into Prudence's food. After she collapsed, unconscious, I dressed her in her pajamas and tucked her into bed, as if she'd had an ordinary night. I left the pills, ordered in her name and with her information on them, on her bedside table, so it would look as if she had bought them and taken them herself. But I was wrong in guessing how much would amount to a deadly dosage."

He had been looking past me, remembering, but now his gaze became focused once more. Glaring at me, he said, "I made the mistake of not finishing the job that night. I won't make the same mistake twice."

He dove towards me suddenly, as if he meant to throw me over the roof. In one swift motion I rolled out of his way, allowing him to lunge past into empty air.

I whirled around just in time to catch a glimpse of Peter sailing over the edge of the bell tower, his desperately flailing hands breaking off a portion of the low railing and dragging it over the side with him.

An instant later, I flinched when I heard the soft 'thud' of his landing below.

Tucker came running over to me. "Are you okay, Emma?"

I nodded, my heart still thundering in my chest. "Just a little shocked," I understated.

Together, we leaned over the broken rail to look at the still figure sprawled below. From here, it was impossible to tell if Peter was dead or just unconscious.

"I've got to get down there," Tucker said, already reaching for the radio clipped to his belt. It seemed that, despite being unarmed and having on his best clothes for the wedding, he was never fully off duty. "I think I heard enough to get the idea of what was going on, Emma," he said. "But later I'm going to need you to explain everything more fully."

"Of course," I said, as he rushed off toward the stairs, already barking orders into his radio.

He interrupted himself only long enough to call over his shoulder to me, "Oh, before Suzy left, she sent me to remind you she needs you at the reception. That's why I came up here."

He raced off down the stairs, before I could answer.

I knew I ought to hurry on over to Suzy. This was still her wedding day and I hoped what had happened wouldn't spoil that. Like almost everyone else, she'd already left for the reception where, with any luck, she'd be so distracted with the festivities that she'd be oblivious to the tragedy that had just played out back here at the church.

Still, I stayed where I was, clinging to the broken railing as I watched Tucker examining the man below. An ambulance pulled into the parking lot only minutes later and, as the emergency workers carried Peter Snipes away on a stretcher, I thought I saw him begin to stir. Not dead then, only injured.

At last I pried myself away from the railing, descended the long set of stairs, and left the old bell tower behind. Hard as it was, I had to bring my focus back to the festivities for just a little longer yet.

As I climbed into the farm truck and drove over to the venue at Shaffers' Farm, it was hard not to feel uneasy. I had pieced together the truth, and I was glad that, even if the worst came to be, at least Prudence's family would know what had really happened. But I was still upset—and not just because a man had nearly died in front of me. I had seen so much strong love between my grandparents and Suzy and Brian that knowing the truth about what Peter did to someone he claimed to love was earth shattering.

When I arrived at the reception, Suzy ran over to me. "Where in the world have you been? Did you get lost?"

I shifted nervously. "Uh, yeah, kind of."

Suzy crossed her arms and raised an eyebrow. "Well, as much as I'd love to hear more about the misadventures of Emma, we have more pictures to take!"

She squeezed my hand and led me over to the rest of the bridal party. I don't think I ever took that many pictures in my life. Poor Billy looked exhausted by the time it was over.

While I was standing at the snack bar afterward, idly chewing on a piece of cubed cheese, Billy approached me with one hand nervously rubbing his neck and the other awkwardly at his side.

Seeing him, it was hard not to blurt the truth out right then and there.

He practically yelled to me, trying to be heard over the music. "Emma, I, uh…"

Suddenly, I realized the question about the wedding that he'd been trying to ask me these past few days. I grabbed his hands and found myself shouting, "Yes, I'd love to dance."

He smiled, looking relieved. "Great! I'd really like that."

As we made our way to the dance floor the upbeat song slowly transitioned to something slower. A love song.

Billy grimaced. "We can wait until after this one if you –"

I wrapped both arms around his neck. "I like this song."

He smiled and put his hands gently on my waist and we slowly moved back and forth to the beat of the music.

The night was one to remember. Everyone was dancing and chatting, and Suzy just glowed the entire evening. Everything was perfect, exactly as she had planned it, maybe even better.

As things were winding down, I found myself walking up to the center of the room to give my obligatory speech. I gripped the paper I had written my notes on and began reading it aloud.

"For those of you who don't know me, my name is Emma

Hooper. I've been best friends with Suzy ever since we grew up together. It has been my honor…"

I hesitated suddenly and looked up at Suzy. Then I crumpled the page in my hand. Suzy's eyes widened, but I flashed her a comforting smile, so she would know I hadn't completely lost my mind.

I explained, "I had a speech prepared, but someone like Suzy deserves so much more than a few planned words. She's not the type of girl you can plan anything out with. She's always changing and growing, and as we all know, she's always been spontaneous. Watching Suzy grow up has been a truly amazing experience. I've never met someone so determined, strong-willed, or – to put it bluntly – bossy."

This raised a few chuckles from the guests.

I continued. "The truth is, Suzy has more often than not been the glue that held us together, and not just the two of us, but our friend Billy as well. The three musketeers. One for all, and all for one. We've all been best friends for as long as I can remember. If any of us ever needed an ear to listen or a shoulder to cry on we were always there for each other. One of our greatest fears has always been losing each other. After all, it takes three people to be the three musketeers. That's just basic math."

A few more polite chuckles came from the audience.

"But now, she has finally found the one who compliments her so well and understands everything about her. She even let him pick out the honeymoon destination! Believe me, I'm as surprised as you are."

This was met with roars of laughter, and one of the groomsmen teasingly tapped Brian's shoulder.

"When I look at Suzy and Brian," I added, "I see a love built on mutual understanding, but more importantly, on trust. I pray you two have a long happy marriage, and that your trust only grows from here on out. Suzy... Suzy, I'm sad to say we are no longer the three musketeers. But Brian..."

I turned my attention to him with a grin. "Brian, I'd like to formally invite you to be a part of the Fabulous Four."

I set the microphone down and rushed out to give the happy couple a hug as all the wedding guests clapped and the crowd began to disperse.

Suzy wrapped her arms around me and grinned in excitement. "Emma, what was that? Your speech was so beautiful."

I hugged her close. "Well, to be honest, the one I had written and prepared was much more poetic and elegant, but I felt like you deserved something more heartfelt."

She laughed. "I loved it and so did Brian! Wait, where's Billy?"

We looked around and saw him hovering nearby.

"Billy, get over here!" Suzy exclaimed.

He came and joined the group hug.

Suzy said, "I love you all so much, every single one of you."

After that, for the rest of the evening, I didn't even have to try to stop thinking about Peter Snipes and my close brush with death. This was a happy occasion for all of us and nothing could spoil it.

CHAPTER 25

"Wow. So it was Peter Snipes all along?" Suzy's eyes were wide. Her white teeth seemed neon against her tanned skin. Brian had arranged for them to honeymoon in the Bahamas, and Suzy had picked up a killer tan over the two weeks they had spent there.

I said, "Yeah, and you know, for a while there I was so sure it was Cindy Green."

Suzy shook her head slowly. "It almost makes you wish it had been Cindy. I mean, a spurned, jealous woman trying to murder a rival is horrible but not so unexpected. But trying to murder someone you supposedly love? Just awful."

It felt so nice to be talking about all of this with Suzy. Of course, I had spilled the beans to Billy practically right away, but I hadn't seen Suzy since the reception and there was no way I was going to ruin her honeymoon that night by telling her what had happened with Peter Snipes back at the church. No, she'd had to wait until she came home to get the story.

I said, "You know, the part I was having the hardest time coping with was that Prudence trusted him. She gave him her heart, and he turned around and tried to kill her. It's almost enough to make anyone want to give up on love. But then I see you and Brian, or my grandparents, and I'm reminded that real, unwavering love is out there."

Suzy wrapped me in a hug. We held each other quietly for a moment until Suzy finally couldn't hold her tongue any longer.

"I can't believe he really tried to kill you, and you still managed to show up to the reception and deliver a speech like *that*. Emma, you are truly amazing."

I laughed. "It was your day. I wasn't about to steal the spotlight."

Suzy's eyes grew wide. "How did Billy react?"

I looked at my hands. "He was shocked, naturally, and annoyed that I hadn't told him about my suspicions involving Peter Snipes sooner. But once I explained my reasons he understood."

I didn't add that I had kept the paranormal nature of my investigation to myself. Billy might know all about the "misfiring synapses" in my brain that allowed me to see ghosts, but I wasn't ready to explain that I could see the spirits of people in comas too—or that I had investigated an attempted murder at the request of a ghost. Even Suzy didn't need to know that.

"What about Tucker?" she asked now.

I sucked in a long breath. "Tucker had a lot of questions. I mean, tons. Honestly, I thought I was never going to leave the police station, after he called me down there the day after the wedding."

Luckily for me, during that meeting with Tucker, I had managed to answer his questions without mentioning ghosts or the fact that I had been intentionally conducting an investigation into what had happened to Prudence. Not exactly being the sharpest tack, Tucker had seemed prepared to accept that I had stumbled onto the truth by accident. The fact that he had arrived in that bell tower in time to overhear Peter Snipes' confession and to see the attempt on my life also simplified matters.

We were interrupted by a knock on Suzy's front door.

Suzy rushed to answer it and, a second later, ushered Billy into the living room. He was smiling and looking relieved, as if a weight had been lifted from him.

"I know Brian's not home right now," he said, "but I figured I'd find you girls together over here. I've just come from the hospital and I have wonderful news that I know you especially will want to hear, Emma."

Suzy and I exchanged glances.

"Well, tell us!" Suzy pressed eagerly.

"It's Prudence Huffler. She's awake."

I stared at him blankly for a moment, unsure of what I had just heard.

Suzy was the first to react. "That's amazing! It's like a miracle, isn't it, Emma?"

It was indeed. A thrill of happiness filled me, as I realized this particular story would have a happy conclusion after all. It was terrible what had happened to Prudence, but she had survived.

"We should send her some flowers," Suzy said, "and maybe visit her, when she's had time to recover her strength."

I nodded, but there was something else on my mind.

"Does she remember anything about what happened to her?" I asked Billy.

"Nothing," he said. "Margene has explained to her about Peter Snipes and she seems to be taking the news pretty well. But she doesn't understand the details yet and of course remembers nothing that happened while she was in the coma."

That last was what I had been waiting to hear. So. Prudence wouldn't recall anything of her visit to me while she was a spirit or of our conversation on that occasion. It was a little sad to think that she was completely unaware of something so important, and yet, in a way I was relieved. It seemed that, at least for a little longer, my secret was safe. Nobody, not even Prudence, need know I was an investigator for the spirits of the dead and dying.

Billy had been saying something to Suzy about the road to recovery that still lay ahead for Prudence. But now he interrupted himself to look at me more closely. "You look distracted, Emma. What are you thinking about?"

I smiled to reassure him. "Oh, nothing. Just thinking of the future," I said.

It was true. Prudence had her life ahead of her again, and now something told me that I too would soon have fresh adventures ahead. I might not know yet what they were going to be but one thing was sure—my future would be ghostly.

* * *

Continue following the ghostly mysteries and eccentric characters of Hillbilly Hollow in "A Dangerous Departure From Hillbilly Hollow."

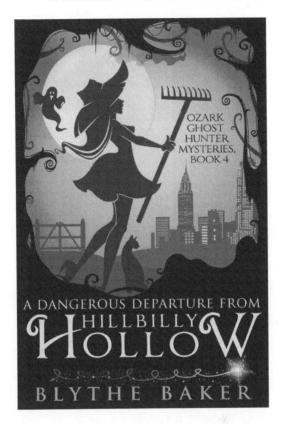

ABOUT THE AUTHOR

Blythe Baker is a thirty-something bottle redhead from the South Central part of the country. When she's not slinging words and creating new worlds and characters, she's acting as chauffeur to her children and head groomer to her household of beloved pets.

Blythe enjoys long walks with her dog on sweaty days, grubbing in her flower garden, cooking, and ruthlessly de-cluttering her overcrowded home. She also likes binge-watching mystery shows on TV and burying herself in books about murder.

To learn more about Blythe, visit her website and sign up for her newsletter at www.blythebaker.com

Made in the USA
Middletown, DE
27 April 2020

92119487R00097